APOCALYPSE THE BETRAYAL

THE POWER OF TWELVE BOOK FOUR

MIRANDA MARTIN

CONTENTS

FOREWORD

Don't miss the start of *The Power of Twelve* start at the beginning if you missed it!

Apocalypse: The Beginning
By Miranda Martin

CHAPTER ONE

AVIELLA

The train car jerks into motion and screams of despair fill my ears as it pulls away. Tears stream down my face. I can't look. People climb on the cars, fighting to get in, desperate to escape.

I can't take it. It's too much. Rafe, Silas, Nate, and Efram close around me, blocking any view out the windows of the posh car the dragons have prepared for us. Even when I cover my ears with my hands, the screams pierce through, stabbing deep into my soul.

My men hold me, supporting me, as the worst decision of my life plays out around us. We've lost people before, I've failed before, but never was it my choice that damned so many souls. It probably isn't long before their screams fade, but it feels like forever.

"Aviella," Nathaniel says, "you made the right choice. We know how hard it was, but it is the only way."

I look at him with puffy eyes, tears running, and sob, shaking my head. He wipes the tears off my cheeks. Rafe kisses one cheek, Silas hugs me tighter, and Efram wraps his arms around my middle, pulling me tight against him.

"What if we're wrong?" I ask, choking on the words that give voice to my fear.

The men look at each other, but no one answers my simple question. I try to find some way to center myself inside the dark of my closed eyes, but even the sanctuary of my own thoughts is a raging black storm.

"I *know* we're not," Nathaniel says at last.

"How can you know that? Is God telling you that? And if he or she or whatever is, then send a message back, would you? I'm done! I can't do this anymore!" I scream, my voice cracking.

I have to break free of their clinging embraces. I can't take it, I don't deserve it. I am solely responsible for the deaths of hundreds if not thousands. How am I any better than the worst of humanity? We could have saved them... somehow.

It's a lie. I know it's a lie I'm telling myself. The Shadow Forces are still too strong, and damn it, they're at least two moves ahead of us. But maybe I could have.

"Aviella," Silas says.

"I want to be alone," I say, motioning them away with a wave of my hand.

The train car is rocking fast, keeping me from running flat out to the door at the rear. I open it and step onto the small balcony. The clacking rattling sound of the steel wheels sliding down the iron rails is deafening, and I welcome it. It's the first thing that comes close to drowning out the sounds of the screams of those I left behind.

After I jump across the gap between cars, I open the door to the next car, slam the door shut behind me and slide down with my back against it. I rest my head between my knees, and I'm overcome by black despair.

"Daddy," I whisper through my tears.

All I want is to save him. I didn't ask for any of this, I'm not special, I'm not strong enough. I can't do this. Why me? Why?

Slamming my fists on the unforgiving steel floor only brings me pain. At least this pain is real. Unlike the throbbing ache that nothing seems to ease, I can do something about it. Rubbing my hands against each other helps, and the heat from the friction feels better and better.

An inferno rages in me, burning through my veins, and as it grows hotter, my magic, that mystical energy I used to think of only as 'it' rises, reacting to the emotional storm. The hair on my arms rises on end and my vision clouds. The world is overlaid with a red haze. I could destroy them all.

Anyone who dares to stand against me or threaten those I have taken under my rightful, righteous protection.

Yes!

Power floods into me, answering my call. I rise to my feet. I raise my hands in front of me. Blue lightning crackles around them and I wiggle my fingers, enjoying the tingling sensation as it plays between the fingertips of each hand, jumping and sparking.

The lightning sparks from me to the walls, ceiling, and floor, and I feel my hair rising as it fills the space around me. I am power. Who could really stand against me?

My anger is a pulsing, throbbing heart of its own. Beating in time to its own drum, ready to rain hell down on my enemies. How dare they stand against me?

Distant cackling laughter reaches my thoughts more than my ears. I try to focus on it, find the source, but every time I almost spot it, it shifts and comes from somewhere else. The magical energy crackles up my arms until it's covering my chest, and my heart pounds. I have to let it go, I desperately need a target, an outlet for the pain, something to be the focus of my rage.

Aviella.

Dad? I turn in a circle. It's him, again.

Aviella, don't give in. You're stronger than this, it's playing you. She's—

His voice is cut off somehow. Even though I only hear it in my head, there's a distinct sensation that he was saying more, and it was stopped, unmistakably. Not by his choice.

I'm empty. Exhausted. With nothing left, I collapse to the floor. The train car's rattling wheels and constant rocking back and forth the only sensations. It's all me. I left them all to die, I can't save my dad, and still, I'm here.

I close my eyes and let the tears fall. With my knees held tight to my chest, sobbing, I cry and I cry and I don't hold back. Grief pours from me until I'm empty. I cry until I'm out of tears. Once I've wiped my eyes dry, I take a deep breath and let it out slowly.

I'm stronger. Dad said it and he's right. I'm stronger—and I must be. The Shadow Forces are coming for me, again and again and each time they come with more, they come harder, and they take more from me. Worse, they've been a step ahead of us every single damn time.

There's a soft knock on the door to the car. After I get up and walk over to it, I rest my head against the cool metal for a second, trying to regain my composure before opening it. When I do, Efram is there, concern on his face.

"Are you okay?" he asks.

"Yeah," I say, stepping back and letting him into the car.

He walks in, and I close the door behind him. His eyes bore into me, soft and yet filled with resolve. Efram. So kind, caring, the most gentle of my men, the rock on which I can always lean.

"You don't have to," he says.

"Have to?" I ask, unsure what he means.

"Be strong," he says, his voice barely above a whisper. "It's okay."

Something lurches in my chest, and I want, for an instant, to throw myself into his arms. Wrap myself up in him and let him protect me from the world and all the hurt and anguish that it brings. Take the decisions off my shoulders, let him tell me it's all okay and believe it.

But it's not. The world is not okay and somehow, for whatever reason, it's on me. The one thing I'm learning, delusional or not, that setting things right is on me. Why, I don't know, nor do I know how. All I know is that it's all coming down to me.

This power I have, it's the only thing that can stop the Shadow Forces. The way they're coming after me leaves no room for doubts about that.

Shaking my head, I smile, if faintly, and square my shoulders.

"It's not, Efram," I say. "It's not going to be until we fix this."

I wave my hands around taking in not the train itself but the entirety of the world. The weight of it lies heavy, but it is what it is.

"Yeah," he sighs, lowering his head. "I know."

He places a hand on my arm, and his magic tingles across my skin, mixing with mine. Our eyes meet and lock as resolve forms. Mine or his, it's impossible to tell, but it flows between the two of us, reinforcing one to the other.

"We'll save him," he whispers. "Soon. We need a base, somewhere safe to form a plan."

"And you think where we're heading is going to be it?" I ask, arching an eyebrow.

His brow furrows and he frowns deeply, pain in his eyes. "No."

"Yeah," I agree. "We're heading into a den of fanatics, but end of the day, that's all that's left it seems."

"What do you mean?" he asks.

An empty feeling forms in my core as my thoughts take shape.

"When it first happened, when all the people disappeared right before the shit hit the fan," I say. "Maybe the ones who disappeared were the... good ones. The well-balanced people. Those who are left, they're all the crazy ones. The ones who are obsessed with... something or someone. They're all fanatics."

It's hard to look at. There's something about it that rings deeply true, not quite a complete truth, or so it feels, but close.

"You mean like the Mega-church?" he asks.

"I mean all of them," I say, sweeping my hand back and forth. "Tynan's bunker they were all obsessed with looks, fashion, getting to be a 'darling'. It was all about their bodies to the point they would harm others or even themselves for any perceived advantage.

"My original bunker, it was all about things, food, credits, it was all stuff. That's what I mean. Have we been anywhere, or have you, that everyone isn't more obsessed with what they want or think they need than they are with being decent to each other? Basic, common human decency left the planet and here we are."

"Aviella," he says, shaking his head, but he doesn't speak a denial.

"Right," I nod, the weight of it all settling onto me until I'm barely able to stand. "That's what we're fighting."

"There are some..." he says, trailing off.

"There are," I agree. "Those are the ones that make this fight worth fighting."

Remembering the good ones, those I've met in my travels and those I know I'll find on the way brings a shadow of a smile. Pushing aside the black despair of my own failures and the overwhelming odds facing us I smile bigger. It's almost like my mouth resists the effort, but I'm in charge here, and I force myself to smile. Then, almost hysterically, I laugh.

Efram's eyes widen, darting around me trying to see if I'm really losing it, I'm sure. That makes me laugh harder. In moments, he's smiling, then chuckling along. I'm laughing so hard, fresh tears form in my eyes. Efram's laughter joins mine, and we let it go. It washes away my fear and my regrets. Well, if not away, pushing them down to a corner.

"Aviella," Efram says, hands on my shoulders, his face an inch from mine as our laughter subsides to soft chuckles.

Impulsively I kiss him. It's chaste, at first, but our energy crackles with a life and desire of its own, turning the soft kiss into something fiery. His arms wrap around my waist, and I throw mine around his neck. Our bodies meld together as he crushes me against him.

Our hips grind against each other, his erection hard and pulsing against my belly. His hands wrap in my hair pulling my head back and he nibbles my ear then kisses down my neck. I moan softly with pleasure. A momentary thought flashes of how wrong this is, knowing what we face, but what am I fighting for and how do I recharge if not finding what pleasure I can?

Efram breaks our kiss and steps back, holding me at arms-length. The fire in his eyes rages, and the bulge in his pants leaves no doubt of his desire. He shakes his head, wets his lips, then swallows.

"This isn't… a good time," he says, glancing at the door we both came through.

He's right. I don't care, but he is. Most of my men, be honest, my lovers are out there. None of us have learned to navigate what we are to each other or how I'm to share them and myself among them. The last thing we need right now is any upset amongst ourselves.

Efram. Sweet, gentle Efram, my angel and my rock.

Touching his face, I nod, unwilling or able to say the words, but he knows. It's on his face and in his eyes. He knows me best of all of them and in many ways, I know him best too.

"I'll be out in a bit," I say, reassuring him with a smile.

He smiles and opens the door to the train car. The clatter of the wheels and the rush of the wind deafens any words we might say, and then he's gone and I'm alone. I lean against the wall, close my eyes, and sigh.

"I don't know who you are, yet," I say softly. "But I will find you. I will kill you. This world isn't yours for much longer."

The faint laughter echoes through my thoughts again, but this time I'm certain it quavers, only a little, but it's there, and I know my enemy is scared.

Good. I'm going to kick its ass.

CHAPTER TWO

SILAS

*W*hen she walks into the train car, the air becomes heavy and electric. It's hard to catch my breath, and it's easy to see I'm not the only one she affects. Conversation stops and everyone turns to look. She stands outlined in the door with magic crackling around her, creating a purple electrical aura. The look on her face is one of resolve.

"We're done," she says.

"What?" Nathaniel asks.

Efram smiles as if he already knows what she's talking about. Rafe sets down the cards on the table as he turns his full attention away from the game he and Nathaniel were playing to pass the time. She looks at each of them in turn, her eyes landing on me last. She's grown, both in maturity and in power.

"We're done," she repeats. "I'm done. We've been a step behind the Shadow Forces all this time. I'm done with it. This is the last bunker, the last time I run. Next time, we fight, no matter the odds. I'm going to find the one behind this, and I'm going to make them pay."

Nathaniel's eyes drop to the ground, Efram smiles, but Rafe tilts his head, staring directly at her.

"The one?" he asks, arching an eyebrow.

"Yes," Aviella says, certainty exuding from her.

"Do we know it's 'one'?" he asks.

The air literally crackles as her eyes darken.

"I do," she says.

"All right," Rafe says, grinning. "Then let's kick this 'ones' ass!"

His attempt at levity falls flat. He looks around the room, grinning, shrugs and picks up his cards. Aviella nods then moves to a cabinet and opens it. She starts looking through the supplies.

"Aviella," I say, walking up to her. "I'd like to do a checkup."

"Why?" she asks, digging through the boxes of supplies. A smile breaks out across her face when she pulls out a box of toaster pops. "Brown-sugar cinnamon!"

"Lovely," I say. "Cardboard with a bit of artificial chemical paste spread between its layers."

"Don't be a spoil sport," she retorts and Rafe snorts.

"I like pop-tarts," Rafe adds.

"You would," Nathaniel says. "I'll call."

The click of plastic chips hitting the table sounds as the two of them continue their game. Those two sitting at a table, being civil, playing cards is, in itself, a testament to Aviella. Who else could bring together an angel and a demon?

"Aviella," I repeat.

"Fine!" she grouses around a mouthful of pop-tart. "Mmm, god, I haven't had one of these since before, when I was a kid."

You're still barely more than a kid, I think to myself.

Yes, she's of age, by modern standards. When I was her

age, she'd have been considered old even, but in the span of years I've walked this earth she's barely a blink of my eye. Yet she draws us all to her. Ensnares us with her beauty, sure, but what is beauty but a fleeting thing? No, it's not the beauty of her flesh that pulls us, it's her soul. She's a bright beacon of righteousness and kindness ensnaring us all.

I lead the way to the far end of the car and into the next where I've set up my things. There are small compartments in these forward cars, each of them packed with as many people as we could save. I reserved a few for our group, but mostly we've commandeered the last few storage cars. I planned it this way to make sure the limited supplies the train could carry are distributed fairly while we journey to the next bunker. Aviella follows me, loudly munching on her treat.

"These are so good, a bit stale, but oh man," she moans.

"How can you tell?" I ask.

"Tell?" she asks, mouth full.

"They're stale?" I ask. "They always seemed stale to me."

"Don't be a spoilsport," she sniffs, then shoves half the so-called pastry into her mouth.

"I'll try," I agree, opening the door and standing to one side so she can enter first.

She waltzes in, dropping crumbs on the carpet as she does. I tense up when I see the mess, but I set it aside. My box of instruments is in the small closet. I dig through it and pull out my stethoscope, hook it around my neck, then I take out a divining rod.

Aviella finishes her treat staring at the tools in my hand.

"Those are different," she comments. "You wanting to play doctor?"

Instantly the energy between us changes. Her magic pulls on me, drawing me to her and the light moment is charged with sexual tension. Her eyelids droop and a smile plays at the corners of her lips and her hips thrust forward the slightest degree.

The attraction is undeniable, I want her, and my body responds in kind. My cock throbs with desire but it's more than that, it's a pulsing, pounding need to be with her. I want to bury myself in her, physically and magically.

It takes all my will to not close the gap between us and take her. This isn't the time.

"Please unbutton your shirt," I order.

Focus. Concentration is my shield, my tower from which I view the world. She unbuttons her shirt, mechanically, pushing aside her own desire the best she can, but her control of it isn't strong. Once the stethoscope in my ears, I place it against her chest, just over the rise of her beautiful breasts.

"Oh!" she exclaims. "Warm it up next time, doc."

"I apologize," I say, my attention absorbed by the sounds coming through the instrument.

It's not only a stethoscope. The carefully inscribed runes on it let me listen to the flow of her magic as it moves through and around her. I close my eyes to hear it better, like the sound of the surf pounding against the white cliffs of Dover.

Her power level has gone up exponentially. I have an idea of what she has yet to face, of the true enemy behind all the attacks, and she'll need every ounce of power she can acquire. There's a rush to the sound that hasn't been there before, and below that there's a hint of sound like a drum. Strange.

I move the scope around to various points on her chest, clinically absorbed in what I'm hearing. The divining rod is next, so I put the scope away.

"What's that?" she asks.

"A divining rod," I say.

"Like you find water with?" she asks.

"Yes," I say.

The rod is about six inches long, I hold it between us and pass it up and down in front of her. I force myself to focus on the rod and not on the way the cloth of her shirt lies over the mounds of her breasts, barely covering the nipples. It's enticing, almost too much so, but the rod in my hand vibrates so I focus on what it's telling me more than what my eyes are telling me to enjoy.

The vibrations change in nature, becoming faster as I move it closer to her chest, slowing when I pass it down to her waist. I continue my examination, gathering in the subtle data the tool gives me.

"Interesting," I say, and put it away.

"Oh yeah?" she asks, placing a hand on my arm.

Her touch is warm, and it momentarily disperses my clinical detachment. It holds my attention with a gravity of its own. The throbbing need of my cock is the only other thing I'm aware of for that instant. My eyes trace a line from her hand, across her shoulder, up her neck, her full pouty lips inviting me to kiss her.

"Yes," I say, my voice throaty despite my attempts to control myself.

She moves her hand up my arm, her touch light as a feather but calling the fire of my pent-up desire, warming me as she passes up to my shoulder, hooking her fingers behind my neck, pulling me to her.

I don't fight her desire or mine. Leaning into her, I put my hands on her waist then jerk her body against mine, letting it meld against me, crushing my ragingly hard cock between us. She rises onto her toes, her body dragging its way against mine, teasing my cock.

Our lips come closer, hers glistening in the soft ambient light. The door slides open behind us.

"Am I interrupting?" Rafe asks.

"Yes," she says.

"No," I say, jumping back.

"Hey, don't stop on my account," Rafe says. "I'm happy to watch. Or join. Either way is cool."

I can hear the grin in his voice, but more than that, I know he means it. The demon has a much different view of sexuality than most. It's his nature as a demon, but I'd wager he wasn't so different as a man. He, of all of us, is having the least trouble with coming to terms with our situation.

She keeps her hands hooked behind my neck. Looking into her eyes, the invitation is there. She's ready and willing but the play is mine. I'm not against it, I want it, but not now. I need to work. There's a lot to do before we reach the Mega-Church Bunker.

I shake my head negative and see the disappointment in her eyes but there's nothing for it. She lets me go and I step back. The space is cramped, so Rafe and I are pressed together as I try to move past him to go out the door. His grin widens when he feels my erection that I can't hide.

"Maybe later," he says with a wink.

Frowning, I push past him into the hall. Outside the window, in the darkness, there's a reddish flash. It's quick, almost too quick for me to notice and entirely too fast for me to discern its source. I stare out into the dark watching to see if it repeats. The terrain flies past, but nothing else happens.

We're making good time though. Tynan was smart, preparing the train ahead. It's the only one I've seen that still has steam power. All the other trains I've seen since the Apocalypse run on human power, but the Dragon Horseman always has plans within his plans. Allowing for escape scenarios in any situation is second nature to him, I'm sure.

Straightening from the window I turn to walk away but bump into Rafe.

"We need to talk," he whispers, looking back to the door where I left Aviella. "Alone."

Nodding I look up and down the train car. Privacy isn't something that's easy to come by. With a frown, I motion towards the front of the car. He frowns too, but then nods. The refugees are up there, but anywhere back here we're likely to be overheard by Aviella.

I lead the way out of this car and step across to the next one up. Despair and apathy wash over me the moment I open the door. It's heavy, hitting me in the chest with a physical force. Rafe puts a hand between my shoulders, steadying me, but doesn't say anything. He feels it too, though as a demon he can draw power from it—not that he does. No, Rafe is different than any other demon I've known.

Their forlorn faces look at us, staring out from the sleeping bunks stacked four high on each side of the train car. Some children play on the walkway, moving about twigs and a partially burnt doll between them. Rafe and I step around them while ignoring the empty faces.

"There were magical scrying traps on the train," he says, pitching his voice for my ears only.

"What!" I exclaim, turning towards him.

"Keep cool," he growls.

The conversations around us stop as all eyes are drawn to my outburst. Damn it, I never lose control like that. Aviella is affecting me more than I care to admit. Grimacing, I nod, and we walk further down the train, neither of us speaking until we're sure that the refugees are no longer paying any particular attention to us.

"What did you find?" I whisper.

"Nate found them," he says, looking around. "Someone bugged the train before we left. Magical scrying devices."

"And?" I hiss.

"And what? We threw them all overboard," he says.

"Good," I say, resolving to double check the train myself.

"Any idea who or what planted them?" he asks.

"I've got a few, but none of them are good," I say.

"I figured as much," he says. "Should we tell her?"

"Not yet," I say. "Keep her busy, I'm going to check the train over and see if I can gather information on the Mega-Church Bunker."

Rafe nods and silently walks away. Some of the refugees are watching me with furtive glances, but I ignore them. They're harmless, for the moment. A tingling on the edge of my awareness pulls my attention, and I look out the window. Almost I think I see that same light play again. Something is watching us, I'm sure of it. Who or what and how I'm not sure of yet. Seems I've got my work cut out for me.

CHAPTER THREE

AVIELLA

I've got too much pent-up energy to sit still. I want to run, move, do something. Anything. But an overcrowded train running at high speed isn't conducive to anything like that. I pace the length of the car again. Nate watches, silent, as I turn an about-face and march back again.

"What do we know?" I muse out loud.

"About?" Nate asks.

"The Mega-church," I snap, not stopping pacing. Nate doesn't answer, and when I glance over my shoulder, he's frowning deeply and staring at the floor. "Nate?"

He shakes his head but doesn't look up. As I turn around to go to him the door behind me opens and Rafe walks in.

"Hey-oh," he sings.

"Nate?" I repeat, ignoring Rafe's entrance.

"What's up with Nate-y boy?" Rafe asks.

"Nothing is 'up' with me," Nate says, rising to his feet. "I have duties to attend to."

He pushes past Rafe then leaves the car. I stare after him knowing beyond a shadow of a doubt he's not telling me something. The only question is why? It's hard to tell with him because I know that sometimes he can't say anything. It's like a mandate from God, or the knowledge is locked from him and he doesn't know but knows. It's weird.

"Well," Rafe says. "Bye."

Rafe turns to me and smiles his devilish grin. Fire burns in his eyes and his magic caresses against mine with an undeniably seductive intention.

"Rafe?" I ask, arching an eyebrow.

My blood sings, rising to his call, as our magic weaves together. He closes with me, wrapping his arms around my waist and pulling me up to meet his lips. Sparks fly as our flesh touches together, literal sparks as our individual magical energies join and his flows into me.

Pleasure sweeps through and I bask in its welcome release for a few moments before I push him back and hold him at arm's length.

"Yes?" he grins. "Too bold? Too fast?"

I roll my eyes and shake my head.

"What are you distracting me from?" I ask.

"Me?" he says, holding a hand to his chest and flourishing the other. "I, madam, am but an innocent demon caught in the flow of fate's mighty hand."

"Right," I say, laughing. "Out with it?"

He smiles and laughs. "I'm passing time. What else do we have to do?"

"We should be planning," I say.

"And what would we plan?" he asks.

"All of it!" I exclaim as the frustration floods back. "How are we going to find the enemy? Where is my dad, how do we save him? How do we save the entire world?"

"Woah," he says, grabbing my hands as I flail them around. "Slow your roll, kiddo."

"This is what I'm talking about!" I say, my voice rising. "It's always slow down, wait. Not yet, Aviella. I'm done with it. All that's gotten us is sitting behind the eight ball at every turn. We've been playing defense and it's high time we went on the offense."

"Sure," Rafe agrees. "We have to start somewhere right? Our next stop is the Mega-Church Bunker. There are Innocents there that we need to rescue, and if I know anything, that place is full of information. They always know more than they're letting on."

"You know?" I ask, curious. "Can you even get in there? I mean, you're a demon."

I'm stating the obvious. I'd assumed he wouldn't be able to go inside with us, considering the nature of the place and what he is.

"Oh how you flatter me," he says, shaking his head. "Yes, I'm a demon. Yes, I can get in there. Why wouldn't I be able to?"

"I don't know, I guess I figured that your kind couldn't get into holy places," I say, cheeks flushing.

Rafe laughs then keeps laughing. Tears pour down his face, he's laughing so hard, holding his sides, and struggling to breathe. I didn't think it was that funny, geez. My skin burns hot and I drop my gaze, glancing around for an escape from the confining space.

"Sorry," he gasps. "Sorry... a minute... oh... yeah, that was good."

"What's good about it?" I snap, my cheeks burning.

"Not you my dear, not really. That place is anything but holy ground. You wouldn't know, it hit me funny that none of us have bothered to tell you."

"Yeah, well thanks for that," I say, crossing my arms over my chest, anger rolling in and flushing away my embarrassment, or at least covering it up.

"Sorry," he says, an abashed look on his face, though with Rafe it's hard to tell. I honestly don't think anything shames him.

"Fine," I say, letting it go. "Tell me what you know." He grins lasciviously, his eyes drifting down my body. "Not that!"

He sighs and shakes his head dramatically. "You're sure?"

"Yes, Rafe," I say. "Come on, I'm trying to be serious."

"See, that's the entire problem, seriousness never got anyone anywhere except in trouble. If you can't have fun along the way, what's the point? Life is a journey, for some of us a damn long one, and if I've learned anything in it, there's no point in being serious."

"You know the odds we face, don't you? The fate of the entire world depends on me!"

"Sure," he nods sagely. "So you can get all 'serious' about it, stress and worry and gnaw on it. Or you can relax, live in the moment, do what you're doing right now, and then deal with the next thing. Never once being 'serious' or 'stressed'. Come on Aviella, don't be Nate and Silas."

"You're impossible," I say, shaking my head as my blood pressure rises.

"Only because I'm right," he says. "Seriously."

His grin spreads from ear to ear when he throws the word back. Against all my own better judgment a laugh slips out.

"Damn it, Rafe," I complain, but I'm laughing now too.

"See, isn't that better?" he asks.

"Fine, now will you tell me what you know?"

"Of course," he says, taking a seat at the table and motioning for me to join him. "The Church bunker is filled with demons."

"Really? Why?" I ask.

"Fear," he says, a solemnity coming over him despite his speech on not being serious.

"What do you mean?" I probe.

"A lot of my kind… feed, for lack of a better word, on fear. There's a lot of fear in that bunker."

"Oh," I say, leaning back in the chair and spinning that around in my mind. "Fear, huh?"

"Yup, place reeks of it," he says.

"You went there?" I ask. "When you were searching?"

Something dark moves behind his eyes but it never touches his face. He picks up the deck of cards and shuffles them doing fancy tricks without once looking.

"I was in the area," he says, deftly dodging the question.

"You can get in, though?" I ask.

"I could, but I won't be inside with you."

"What? Why not?"

"I'll be outside, standing guard. The Shadow Forces will try to grab you there. If they'll attack Tynan in his home bunker, then there is no doubt in my mind they won't hesitate to go after you here. Only this time, I'll be waiting for them."

"That's a horrifying idea," I say.

"Oh?" he asks, arching an eyebrow.

He waits, silent, for me to present a counter, and it hits me how much my relationship with the men has changed in such a short time. It wasn't that long ago they wouldn't have listened to my objections to anything, knowing they knew better than I did. They did, too. I'm not stupid or too blind to admit that. Now, they at least listen when I have a counter.

"You can't be alone outside, they'll take you out before any of us would have a chance to help you. What good would that do anyone? You should be at my side, strength in numbers."

"Your logic is sound," he says. "The thing is, I have certain skills that I can't bring to bear inside the bunker as easily as I can outside. Trust me, they won't find me before I'm ready, and I'm not going to take them on single-handedly. I'm not that kind of hero."

"Good," I say, placing my hand on his, forcing him to stop shuffling. "I can't lose you."

Magic crackles to life, ringing our hands, racing across our skin. The hair on my arms stands on end and my mouth is dry while my lower parts seem to pull all the moisture from my body.

"You can't lose me," he says, his voice husky. "Ever."

The pull between us is magnetic, drawing me into him. All my pent-up energy rises to the fore, magnifying my magic.

"Rafe—" I say, but he cuts me off with a kiss.

His lips move against mine, magic roiling inside and outside of us, flowing from him into me and back like some crazy circling river except it keeps amplifying. I give myself over to him, accepting his energy as I accept his body.

He retreats, leaving us breathless. I'm gripping the edge of the table, leaning into him, empty except for aching desire. The dragon's fire in my blood roars to life, and I grab the front of his shirt, pulling him to me, our lips smashing together.

His tongue drives into my mouth, and I open to welcome it. The fire burning through into him. When we break this time, we're both leaning over the table between us, panting.

"Aviella," he says, panting, then shakes his head. He takes my hands in his, and his eyes shift to black with red streaks through them.

Suddenly we're no longer on the train, but standing together in an open field under a brilliant night sky. The grass is green around us, there are trees and even the sound of birds singing in the distance. Staring wide-eyed, I kneel and run my hands through the grass. It feels real.

"Rafe..." I say, trailing off without further words.

"Nice, huh?" he asks.

"It's... beautiful," I say, unable to stop touching the grass. "How... where..."

"It's not real," he says, a note of sadness in his voice. "An illusion, a bit of a dream."

"It's incredible," I say, digging my fingers into the dirt and then running them through the soft blades. "How?"

His smile broadens as he kneels next to me. "Illusions are part of my abilities. I am, my dear, a demon after all."

He touches my face, lifting my chin up until our eyes meet, then he leans in and kisses me. It's a surprisingly tender, soft kiss, filled less with the burning passion and desire I'm used to from him, but something so much more. It's filled with love.

Love. It's an entirely different fire, but one I welcome. I return his gentle kiss, then wrap my arms around his neck and pull him into me. Falling back on to the soft grass, illusion or not, his body presses against mine and we keep on kissing.

"Rafe," I gasp, breaking for air.

"Shhh," he whispers, his hands grasping the fastener of my pants and deftly undoing it. "Not now."

Thoughts are pushed aside as his hand slides over my mound and parts my wet, waiting lips with a finger. I shudder as he passes over my clit then curls up inside.

After pushing my tongue past his lush lips, seeking his, I explore his mouth as his fingers explore my soft folds. While I dig my nails into his back, I gasp as he finds a spot that creates tiny nuclear explosions of pleasure throughout my body.

The dragon's fire I've taken from my melding with Tynan roars through my limbs, burning my veins, demanding I take control and take him.

I can't resist it. my legs wrap around his hips and I buck

up, twisting as I do and forcing him to roll over with me. From on top of him I arch my back and grind my hips, forcing his fingers deeper inside to fill the aching emptiness.

I run my fingers through my hair, thrusting my chest out, and grinding, groaning with pleasure. Rafe laughs, a soft, enticing chuckle welcoming my actions.

He uses his free hand to undo his pants then slides the hand up under my shirt, seeking my tits. When he grabs the mound of soft flesh and thumbs my nipple, it's my turn to laugh.

"Rafe," I groan, grinding my hips faster against him.

I fumble with his pants and underwear until his generous, uncut cock is free. I'm not waiting for anything. I guide it immediately in to replace his fingers, filling my void.

As I settle onto him with a satisfying sense of fullness, I push down until he's fully seated inside. Holding myself there, I bite my lip, close my eyes and enjoy the sensation of his girth filling me. He grabs my shirt and rips it open, buttons flying away, then grabs my tits and squeezes them tight.

It's almost painful but balanced out by the depth of pleasure from his dick. We hold, neither of us moving, breathing and letting the sensations escalate on their own. Slowly he pushes his hips up forcing me to lean forward which causes my clit to grind against his pelvis.

"Oh!" I exclaim as my sensitive nub hits sensation overload.

Stars dance behind my closed eyelids. Biting my lip I shift slowly back and forth, increasing the pressure on my clit and making his cock shift inside of me. He takes both nipples under his thumbs and circles them before driving himself up into me, hard.

It's more sensation than I can process, and primal instinct takes over. We hump and thrust with each other, our bodies finding their own rhythm and taking me along for the ride. Pleasure comes in ever-building waves, pushing me higher as my core tightens with each thrust he makes.

I don't know how long it goes, but it builds and builds.

"I'm going to come," I gasp, eyes closed, fingers tensing as the orgasm rips through me

My toes curl, my back arches, every muscle tightens as it rocks its way through my body, clenching everything tight. My pussy clamps on his dick and I feel him exploding into me, pumping over and over.

As it passes, my muscles relax and I collapse onto him, my arms too weak to keep me up.

Our chests press against each other, and I feel his heart pounding against me, almost in time with my own rapid beating. He turns his head towards me, his warm breath passing over my neck making me shudder, then he nibbles my ear.

"Oh, too much," I say and laugh, pulling away from him.

I roll off the top of him and lie next to him, still trying to catch my breath.

"I've been told that before," he says, grinning like the devil he is.

"Not that," I roll my eyes. "That was perfect, you dolt."

"I know," he says, nodding.

"You're impossible," I say.

"I've been told that too," he says. "Though normally it's followed by 'good', at least after making love."

Staring up at the beautiful, starry sky, illusion or not, I wait for my heart to slow, concentrating on the rhythm of my body. Something is different. I can't put my finger on it yet, so I listen and wait.

There. I spot something, a feeling or almost a stray thought, but I have to chase it down. My magic flows through my body with a cyclic wave, one I'm used to, but every time I've joined with one of my men it's changed as I take a piece of them into me.

What have I gained from Rafe, though?

He rolls onto his side, propping his head up on one arm, trailing the fingers of his free hand along my stomach. I shiver as he hits a ticklish spot, trying to ignore him until I trace down the difference I'm feeling. When I don't respond to his satisfaction, he lowers his head and kisses his way down starting right under my breasts.

"Rafe, wait," I wiggle under his ministrations.

"Hmm?" he asks, not stopping lavishing my skin with his tongue.

I've almost got it, but it keeps slipping away. Something has changed. He's on my lower stomach kissing across my belly button and then he starts lower. He places his hands on my thighs, forces my legs open, and lowers himself between them right as I'm about to figure it out.

His hot, rough tongue blasts it away and my back arches up again. I twine my fingers in his hair to pull him tight against me, pushing him up and down as he works magic. As if on cue, my magic and his sparks together and blue lightning races around my limbs, encircling his head.

He works his tongue frantically and I'm pushed towards a new orgasm faster than I ever would have thought possible. The magical energy ignites every single nerve ending. He shoves two fingers in at the same time he flattens his tongue roughly against my clit, and I'm rocked by my own orgasm controlling my body.

I cry out in pleasure as he grabs my ass and holds me tight against him. My body convulses multiple times until the last of my pleasure is spent and I collapse once again. Gently he kisses his way up my belly then lies down beside me. I rest my head on his chest and let my fingers trace along the hard lines of his muscles.

Now, relaxing, I can feel the magic flowing through the two of us like we're two conduits feeding each other. His magic is so different from the others, which doesn't really surprise me. I've joined with enough of them now to know that they are each unique. The most surprising thing with his is that it's peaceful. I would expect this more from Nate, as an angel, than from the demon.

My own magic pulses now with a steady, gentle beat that is evened out by his joining it. I'm calm. I've been resolved, but now there's more to it than resolve. All the pent-up energy feeling and the need to be in action is now replaced with this acceptance of being where I am.

"Talk to me," I say.

I move my fingers down lower, lightly teasing his soft cock which stirs to my touch.

"About?" he asks.

"What was it like, for you before?" I ask.

"Heh," he chuckles. "You want a look into the darkness, do you?"

"I find it hard to think of you as ever being 'dark,'" I say, listening to the steady thrum of his heart and his breath.

"Yeah, well," he sighs. "All of us have a past."

He shifts, rising up to a sitting position and forcing me off his chest. I sit beside him, tilting my head and waiting while he stares into the distance.

"What is it, Rafe?" I ask.

"You," he says, looking at me. "Aviella, it's you."

He's not the first one to say something like this to me, but I don't think I really understand it. I'm not special. I'm an orphan lost in the Apocalypse. Sure, I've got magic and that sets me apart, but I don't *feel* special.

It puts me on a spot, like I'm on a pedestal. The feeling is the same as one of those dreams you have where you go to school and only when everyone is laughing and pointing at you do you realize you're naked.

"If you say so," I say, shaking my head.

"And that, my dear, is exactly it," he says, placing two fingers on my cheek and pulling my eyes back to his. "You don't see it. If you did then you'd probably be as arrogant as... well, me."

He grins, shaking his head.

"Well, that would be something wouldn't it?" I say. I laugh, letting it all go.

There's a preternatural calmness that I'm experiencing, and for the moment, at least, I want to hang on to it. Rafe rises to his feet, grabbing his clothes. The grass and stars above flicker like the shadows cast by a candle's flame.

"We should go," he says. "This takes a lot of juice to maintain."

Nodding my agreement, I dress too.

CHAPTER FOUR

AVIELLA

The train rattles constantly as it rolls down the tracks. A clickety-clack sound creating a white noise that I only notice when I first wake up. When I stretch out, my feet hit the wall at the end of my bunk, and the wall at my head keeps me from stretching my arms that way. Grunting, I roll out and drop to the floor.

The boys have given me a private room. A luxury, for sure. The train is overcrowded with survivors everywhere else. Well, it's private, yes, but it's also loaded to the gills with supply boxes, which makes it almost impossible to get a good stretch.

Ugh. Rubbing my face, I weave through the stacks of boxes, open the door, which is only wide enough for me to slide out sideways, and walk the few steps down to the dining area. Nate is sitting at the table staring intently at a scroll in his hands. He doesn't even look up when I walk in.

"Morning," I say.

"Good morning," he says, still staring.

Okay then, obviously he's absorbed with whatever that is. Curious, I walk over and stand behind him to look at the paper. It's covered with a flowing script done in some kind of silver ink that almost glows. I've been around long enough now to recognize angelic script when I see it. There's a hint of power in the script as well that makes my skin tingle.

"Angelic orders?" I ask.

He grunts then as if only now realizing I'm looking over his shoulder. He rolls the scroll up and slides it inside his jacket.

"Do you want breakfast?" he asks, rising to his feet and pointedly ignoring my question.

"Sure," I say, watching him as he goes to a cabinet and rummages through the supplies.

I'm not angry. Which is weird. Normally I'd be upset, irritated at the very least, if not flat-out pissed at his behavior. Today I'm not. Looking this over, I decide it's not a bad thing. In fact, I like it. It's a more detached view and that's good.

Obviously, there's information on there he doesn't want me to know. It may be personal or something else, but I trust Nate, even if he can be the most frustrating man I've ever met. Except for Silas. Those two compete for the crown when it comes to being frustrating.

I know Nate won't let any harm come to me, and he's always working for the greater good. Despite the fact he's an angel, which I've learned the hard way isn't any indicator of goodness. If anything, an angel is more likely to be cold, calculating, and have no concerns for those in front of them. The entire Apocalypse has been orchestrated at least half by their hands after all.

Nate pulls out some nutri-rations—boring, plain but filling. He lays them out on the table, and we sit down together and eat. Restlessness fills me like buzzing gnats. A desire to move, to be in action hits me so strong that my leg is bouncing.

"Problem?" Nate asks.

"No," I say, shaking my head. "Yes. I don't know."

He arches an eyebrow, chewing a bite of rations and waiting.

"What is it?" he asks, after I don't answer.

"I think I'm going to check on the refugees," I say.

"I did that a few hours ago, they're fine," he says before taking another bite off the pressed ration bar. "They're tense but physically okay."

Biting my lip, I frown and nod to his words.

"Sure," I agree. "I need to do... something. Anything besides sitting here waiting."

Nate gives me a rare smile, one that shows his understanding. Shoving the last bit of my ration bar into my mouth, I get up and head towards the next car. As I step across the platforms between cars, my attention is drawn out to the view rushing past.

The landscape is a hell of its own unique design. Remnants of trees reach for the sky like skeletal fingers, stripped of their bark and blackened by fires. The land is mostly flat, and I wonder where we are, exactly. Or where it was before the Apocalypse. Now it's here and that's all that really matters isn't it?

The instant I open the door to the next car, a wave of oppression hits me in the chest, making it hard to breathe. I grab the railing to brace myself before pushing past it and entering the crowded car. Forlorn faces look out at me from the stacked bunks, empty and scared.

Whispers follow as I walk down the aisle. A gaunt-looking woman with a little girl looks out of her bunk as I approach. Something about her calls my attention, so I stop and kneel.

"Hello," I say.

The corners of her mouth twitch but don't form a smile.

Her eyes are dull and lifeless. The child clings to her, and it's more than fear rolling off of them, it's despair. Black and empty, no hope for the future. When I touch her face, a shock runs up my arms, causing a constriction in my chest and a pain in my heart.

Magic rises in response to the influx, buzzing as it takes hold of the negativity. Light-headed, I shift my feet to keep from falling over. The woman's eyes brighten, and the twitching of her lips becomes a real smile. The whispers behind me grow louder.

"Thank you!" the woman exclaims.

A tingle runs up and down my arms then across my chest. The refugees push in, closing on me. Hands touch me from all sides. Each touch is one of despair, loss, and grief. It flows into me like a river of blackness.

I'm pushed from side to side while I'm being crushed both physically and spiritually. Turning my head, trying to find a way out—there are so many desperate people. Their angst is trying to rush over me. It's too much, I can't take it all, but their despair continues to flow into me, over-whelming.

There's not enough room to breathe, can't expand my lungs, can't think. Panic rises, awareness contracts to noth-ing. Get out of here, I have to get free!

Suddenly the stars are above me and I'm in the middle of the open field as I was with Rafe last night. Calm, in control, unable to be affected by the world outside.

My magic burns hot like a bonfire, and it consumes their emotions, drinking them. Their despair is oxygen to its flames. The crowd stops pushing in as they each return to their bunks. All their eyes are on me. Some talk softly to those next to them, and they whisper my name.

I bask in their admiration as power surges through me then I stumble. They watch, silent, waiting for me to do something but what I don't know. A deep sense of satisfaction wells inside. They want me to say something but my cheeks flush hot. This isn't me. I'm not a public speaker.

"Be well," I say, awkwardly.

"She said be well," various voices whisper.

I keep my eyes on the door through the spinning in my head, brace myself with hands on the walls, and stumble my way out. Escape their hungry gazes. The door closes behind me and I take in the first deep breath I've had since walking in. What in the name of all the devils was that?

Gripping the railing tight, I gasp in the warm night air. The hair on my arms stands on end, and it feels like I can't get a deep enough breath. Magic races through me, out and around, coming back in like it's on a feedback circuit growing with each pass through. I helped, I think. I'm not sure what I did, but I need a shower. Everything feels icky.

Nathan is gone from the table, so I go right to the showers. I let the warmish water wash over me, trying to not think about what happened. It's impossible not to, of course.

It's not that it was bad. What I did helped them, I think. The thing is, what was it I did? What was that sense of... fulfillment? Satisfaction? Whatever it was I felt after I did it. That holds my attention, no matter how much I don't want to look at it.

Their despair was a feast, and I gorged myself on it. I shiver and not just because the water is ice cold, so I step out and grab a towel. The help I gave is good, but the way it happened bothers me. I liked it. A lot. Even thinking about it makes my skin tingle and there's a hunger for more.

I dress quickly and go to join the boys. As I get closer the smell of coffee and nutri-meal is on the air and my stomach rumbles. That's a sensation I can get on board with!

"Hey!" Rafe says, grinning as he lays a steaming bag out on a bowl in the middle of the table.

Efram deftly opens it with a small dagger and the odor of it fills the car. It's a fake, chemical scent but this is what I grew up on, and I'm much more used to it than the grandiose affairs Tynan served.

"Hi guys," I say, taking my place at the table next to Efram.

Silas sits at the head of the table and Nate is at the opposite end. Glancing between the two of them I snort.

"What is it?" Efram asks, arching an eyebrow.

"Nothing," I say, really laughing now, unable to contain it.

"It seems like more than nothing," Rafe chimes in as he pops another meal pack into the microwave.

My cheeks warm and I can't look at any of them, my eyes water and I keep laughing.

"Aviella," Silas says, in his serious voice. "Would you not care to share your amusement with the rest of us?"

His words play into the image in my head which makes me laugh even harder.

"It's good she's laughing," Nate says. "Let her be, Silas."

I guffaw loudly, and my laugh starts to sound like a hyena. God this is so embarrassing! I can't stop, gasping air and slapping the table as I struggle to get control. Efram rubs my back, trying to help.

"Aviella," he says, whispering into my ear. "Are you okay?"

The concern in his voice is clear and helps to stall out the manic laughter.

"Yeah," I gasp, shaking my head and wiping the tears away. The boys watch with expectant faces, so I explain. "It struck me that we're a family."

They look at each other in obvious confusion, but no one speaks to contradict me though it's obvious they don't see why it's so funny.

"Well, all righty then," Rafe says, turning back to the microwave and pulling out another steaming bag.

He doesn't bother to use an oven mitt. His bare hands are immune to the heat, I guess. Perks of being a demon. No one says anything more but they're all looking at me waiting to see if I'll explain. My cheeks are hotter than the steaming bag on the table, but I can't leave them hanging.

"Silas is at the head of the table," I explain, "so he's the Dad, Nate you're the Mom and Efram, Rafe and I are the kids."

It sounds stupid when I say it out loud but that was the image that popped in my head. Now they're staring and I want to crawl under said table and hide. Then Rafe busts out laughing, doubling over with the force of it and Efram is grinning, trying to contain himself.

Silas chuckles, shaking his head followed by Efram's laughing out loud. Only Nate is left staring without laughter. I bite my lower lip waiting for his response.

"I'm the mother?" Nate asks.

Slowly, I nod that he's right. He frowns, his brow furrowing, then he nods too.

"I suppose I am," he agrees.

Rafe turns purple he's laughing so hard, and then Silas laughs out loud too. I'm laughing again as Nate shrugs and grabs the bowl of food dipping some onto his plate. Stoic as ever. Efram laughs politely but it's obvious he's not in the spirit of it all.

I take my place at the table, wiping away the tears of my laughter. It's good to have these moments of relief—they're all too brief. As we eat, the familiar weight slowly settles onto my shoulders. We're racing across the blasted landscape to our next destination. It's time we had a plan, or if they have one that they tell me about it.

"Coffee?" Efram asks, rising from the table.

"Please," I reply, picking up my cup.

He pours coffee for everyone, then resumes his seat. The

meal is ending leaving five of us sitting in a stiff silence. No one speaks, but we're all looking around with what looks to me like furtive glances at each other. It's awkward, and I don't like it. This isn't the way it should be, isn't the way it needs to be. Like I have a clue what that supposed to be is, but I do know this doesn't feel right, and what else do I have to go on?

"I should go," Nate says, rising from the table, not meeting my eyes.

"We need a plan," I say, stopping him mid-rise.

"A plan?" he asks.

"Yes, a plan. I told you all, I'm done reacting. I'm done with being one step behind. We need a plan, one that puts us ahead of whoever or whatever our actual enemy is."

Nate sits back down, pursing his lips, hand balling into a fist on the table.

"Do you have one?" Silas asks.

"No," I admit. "I don't. What do we know?"

I look at each one of them in turn, holding eyes with Silas the longest. He doesn't flinch or look away from my stare. His eyes have that soft shade of green that's almost brown but not. They're deep pools of careful observation that weigh and measure all he sees without comment.

"Well…" Rafe says. "Things are changing in the Underworld. Something's happened or happening and my contacts, normally talkative things that they are, are shutting up."

"I'm seeing the same," Nate agrees. "On the other side, of course."

"The dead are restless," Efram says quietly.

He doesn't talk often about his own skill set, especially around the others. I admit it's creepy but having developed similar powers myself it's damn useful.

"Silas?" I ask, since he's the only one who hasn't contributed.

36

He purses his lips then rubs the bridge of his nose, sighing.

"There have been disturbances that I'm aware of, yes," he says. "None of this is surprising. Another Trumpet has sounded. I would be more surprised if things weren't changing."

"It's more," Rafe says, leaning his elbows on the table and looking thoughtful. "Something big, something is moving, consolidating power."

"My side suspects as much, from what I can gather," Nate says.

"Who? Or should I ask, what?" I ask.

"Six of one, half a dozen of the other," Rafe chuckles but it's a forced sound even for him.

"Right," I say. "So what do we do? What else do we know?"

"The Dragons are our strongest ally," Silas says. "Thanks to you Aviella, I'd say they are firmly on our side. Three of the four anyway. We need the fourth. If we can free Casmir…"

"What?" I ask, looking around, but none of them meet my eyes.

Rafe holds up his hands, shaking his head. Nate stares at the table and Efram looks out the window. Magic crawls across my skin making the hair on my arms stand on end. The buzzing inside of me grows, making me feel antsy.

"Casmir isn't like the other three," Rafe says. "I've dealt with him."

"He's mad," Efram whispers. "Obsessed with his 'projects'. Salvaging him is a long-shot."

"Projects?" I ask.

"He's what you would consider a mad-scientist," Silas says.

"You're kidding, right?" I ask, incredulous.

37

"No, I don't kid," Silas says.

"Of course you don't," I mutter. "Rafe? What do you know?"

"He's dark," the demon says, quite a statement, considering. "But hey, we've faced dark odds before, so why not? Let's salvage the mad-scientist Horseman, why not?"

Rafe grins, his boyish charm coming off of him in waves. Nate looks at Rafe and shakes his head. Efram sighs and Silas clears his throat.

"It won't be easy," Silas says. "But I'm sure we'll figure it out. I don't think we'll have a choice."

"What about Tynan?" I ask.

When I say his name it echoes through my soul, as if it's pinging the connection I have to him. The dragon magic I've absorbed from him roars to life, burning through my veins. I shudder as it races up my spine and clouds my thoughts.

I could dominate all of them, none of them are on my level. I am better than all of them together. They should all be dancing to my will. Closing my eyes I fight against the base instincts that come along with his magic. Damn it, Tynan, quit being an asshole.

"I would not count on his assistance for this one," Silas says. "The brothers are not close from what I know."

"Anybody else?" I ask, looking around for more input.

One by one they shake their head.

"Great," I mutter, rising to my feet.

I'm restless, again, and there doesn't seem to be any point in continuing this conversation.

"Hey," Rafe says. "We'll figure it out. Hang on to that."

"Yeah, sure," I say, irritably. "We'll get by on a hope and a prayer."

"Sometimes, prayer is the best resource," Nate says softly.

I whip around to face him, a sour retort on the tip of my

tongue but it dies when I see the sincerity on his face. The dragon magic subsides, relinquishing its control.

"Yeah, I only wish it was more…. Reliable," I say.

"I understand," Nate says, head bowed and shoulders slumped.

CHAPTER FIVE

NATHANIAL

*P*ausing at her door I take a moment to try and bring myself under control. The sense of her caresses me through the thin wood of the door. Even this close she affects me. She's a siren's song, calling me closer, tempting me with the sweet pleasures of the flesh, but it doesn't stop there. No, it's so much more than flesh.

Her magic grows every day, we all feel it, and struggle to hold our own against it. It's unclear where this is going, but I can't deny my feelings. My life is duty, obligation, dedicated to the Creator, God as she would call him. I'm an angel, made to serve. We do not have free will like the humans, or the demons. When the Call comes, I will serve. There is no question of that, but between the times of a Call I am my own man.

My own man who struggles with my own inherent weaknesses. Ones I did not know I had until her. Everything about her is intoxicating. I can't give in to those desires, not now. I need to help her, mold her, shape her toward the destiny I sense, even if I can't see it, at least not yet. I have no doubts that it will be revealed to me when it's time.

I center myself by inhaling deeply and then knock on the door.

"Come in," she calls.

Aviella is sitting on the edge of the bunk bed, surrounded by boxes of food and other supplies. This space is tight, but it's the best we could arrange for her to have some privacy. She's going through a lot, learning her magic, dealing with those of us who are falling for her, and coming to terms with her own destiny. It's the least we could do.

She's leaning over, resting her arms on her legs. I can't stop my eyes from noticing the exposed cleavage where her shirt is not fully buttoned. The soft creaminess of her skin, the rise and fall of her breasts as she breathes. She's staring at the floor, hair falling around her face, creating a tunnel that leads straight to those gentle mounds.

My cock stiffens and my thoughts spin, becoming primal. Breathing heavily I grab myself mentally and force the urges down. I will not give in to them.

"Would you like to train?" I ask, forcing my voice to be steady, holding myself back from crossing the small space and taking her in my arms.

"Why?" she says, shaking her head.

"What happened in the car," I ask. "Earlier, when you checked on them. What happened?"

She doesn't say anything, but I notice a slight shiver. "Nothing."

"Aviella, do not lie to me," I say, forceful.

Her head snaps up and her beautiful eyes tinge red, her lips curl back into a snarl.

"Do not threaten me," she growls.

Interesting. I hold up my hands palms out keeping my face composed.

"No threat, Aviella," I explain. "I can't help if I don't know."

The anger and rage is gone as fast as it came. Her cheeks flush before she can hang her head again hiding her face behind her hair.

"Sorry," she says. "It was... nothing."

"Nothing?" I probe. She shakes her head but doesn't say more so I probe. "What kind of nothing? Why does nothing bother you?"

She sighs heavily and leans back onto the bed, placing her arms to hold herself up. I can't help but notice the way her legs are spread, opening her core. Exposing herself to me. It shouldn't be erotic, she's fully clothed as am I and its clear she's not intending anything by the position, but nothing seems to stop my thoughts from going there.

"They... need something," she says, shaking her head. "They're so... heavy is the best way I can describe it. Laden with negative emotions. Weighted down and desperate for relief."

"They've lost everything," I agree.

"Yeah," she says, twisting around and pulling her legs up under herself. I'm quietly thankful for it, it makes keeping my concentration on her much easier. "I suppose, it's nothing."

She glances up, meets my eyes for an instant then turns her head to look out the small window at the darkening landscape sliding by outside.

"I did not mean that your experience was nothing," I say, holding myself back from crossing the room.

I'm afraid if I take her in my arms right now, I won't be able to stop myself. It's ridiculous. I can't offer her the small measure of comfort that is a hug without worrying I might lose control and turn it into something so much more. Now is not the time.

"I know," she agrees. "It's fine. What's up? Why'd you want to train?"

She's changing the subject and for a moment I debate not allowing it. I could probe, push her to tell me what's happening but no. She is growing into her own power, I have to let her. Our relationship is changing. If I don't allow it, if we don't, none of us are likely to survive.

"Silas says you're ready," I offer.

She turns back from the window, a grin on her face. "Oh boy."

Smiling I nod. "Your power is growing. I can teach you new symbols, new methods of fighting."

"Good," she says, the grin disappearing. "I have to be ready."

"May I?" I ask, motioning to the end of the bed.

"Of course," she nods, scooting more to the head of the bed.

I take a seat and sit down, cross legged in front of her. She mimics my position. Taking her hands in mine I close my eyes and project us into the astral. She follows me, coming along on her own power. On the astral plane we have room to work, unlike back on the train.

She turns in a circle, looking around the space I've prepared for us. She bites her lower lip and the urge to kiss her causes me to shudder as I struggle to control it.

"Nice wards," she says, noting the magic I've inscribed around us.

"Thank you," I say. "Follow along."

I move my hands through space to draw out the first of the symbols in the air. Silver energy forms the lines as I draw them, connecting each piece until the symbol is a blinding white design that looks like a Gordian knot drawn in the air overlaid with an infinity symbol.

Aviella follows along, faltering part way through and her glowing lines break apart with a puff of silvery light and a hint of cinnamon on the air.

"Damn it," she curses, eyes flashing red.

Dragon magic fills the air between us, passing over me in waves, tinged with anger. My own magic rises against it, resisting and then suddenly on a magical level the two of us are locked against each other. Her face darkens as the color of her eyes takes on a reddish-black tint.

"Aviella," I say, pulling back my magic.

She stops instantly, magic dropping away as fast as she stops the flow of her anger and power.

"Sorry," she says, shaking her head.

"Tynan?" I ask.

She flushes and nods, biting her lip again.

"His magic is… volatile," she says. "If I don't watch myself, it jumps ahead of my control."

"I understand," I say. "Try again."

We set to work. Time on the astral is slower than what is passing in the real, so we have plenty of it. She works the design again and again until, faster than I ever could have expected, she masters it. The symbol glows in front of her, pulsing with power.

"Good!" I exclaim.

She smiles and nods. "It was easy once I figured this part out."

She points to where the lines knot and I nod. That is a tricky part of the symbol.

"Prepare yourself," I say. I close my eyes and will attackers into existence.

Magic coalesces making the equivalent of magical golems. Two mimics of the undead monstrosities we've fought appear and shamble towards her. She watches them approach, unperturbed as she would once have been. As she turns her head to each of them the symbol moves with her gaze. The monsters close with her, holding her attention.

I create a gargoyle behind her, hovering in the air a dozen

feet up. As the two monsters rush in to attack, the gargoyle dives for her. Pure white magic forms around her hands, and she raises them to defend against the approaching undead.

The gargoyle is almost to her, long clawed hands reaching for the back of her neck. In a blur of motion she swings her arms up and out. White magic flashes, and the symbol she's drawn in front of her whizzes behind, shielding her from the gargoyle. It touches the symbol and explodes into a puff of gray dust.

She doesn't stop moving. She swings her arms that are raised overhead down and around in a flowing motion, bringing the symbol with her. It cuts through the undead and they too explode into gray dust. She straightens, staring at me.

"Tricky with the gargoyle," she says.

"Battle is tricky," I say, and she nods her understanding.

I'm in awe of how fast she's learned this symbol. I've taught new angels this one and it's hours before they master it. She's absorbed it and wielding it like a pro in a comparative blink of an eye.

"This is good," she says, staring at the design. She frowns, her head tilting to one side. "Shield?"

"You can read it?" I ask, unable to keep the surprise out of my voice.

"Sure," she shrugs as if it's nothing. She shouldn't be able to. It's angelic script, how can she read it? "It's not easy, but I get it."

"Okay, continue," I say, creating illusions to challenge her more.

I create them as fast as I can and she keeps up, longer than I expect before she shows signs of wearing down. She wields the new symbol deftly, using it with the skill of someone long practiced in angelic magic.

She's surrounded by a mob of illusory undead, all

reaching for her, when I add in a trumpet beast. A mutated crocodile, three heads filled with sharp teeth, so big it towers over the mob surrounding her. Its bulbous yellow eyes lock onto her.

She gasps and steps back, which is a mistake. One of the undead illusions gets a hold in her hair and jerks her off her feet. She falls backwards. Her hands glow bright white as the mob piles over her, burying her from my sight.

Instinctively I move to stop the illusions, but then I wait, holding off to see what she will do if this situation happens in a real battle. How will she react? Our enemies are legion, I must prepare her. My chest constricts, wings rustle, and it's hard to breathe, but I let it play out.

She screams, the sound cutting through the moans and growls of the monsters. My heart aches, and the desire to help her, to save her, is so strong it takes all my will not to. She will not become what she must, will never find her true purpose and fulfill her potential if I do not push her. No, this is the right thing. No matter how difficult.

I split my attention to look at her body in the material realm while watching her struggle on the astral. Her body is stiff, back ramrod straight, sweat pouring down her face. She grits her teeth, and through the mob on the astral plane surrounding her, a white glow brightens. The monsters' growls edge higher, turning to something else. In a moment the growls are howls of pain.

Suddenly the pile of monsters blasts off of her, exploding into a mess of parts. She's left hunched over on the ground covered in blood and guts. She looks up, eyes burning white with red centers. She locks eyes with the trumpet beast and now she growls. Her right hand balls into a fist, while her left weaves through the air, forming the symbol I just taught her.

The monster moves, snapping in with all three heads at once. She raises the shield, slamming it into the thing's body below the heads, stopping it from reaching her. Her right hand thrusts forward and raw power explodes outward, blasting into the thing. It explodes into millions of pieces, dispersing into dust. Aviella collapses, dropping to the ground then out of the astral.

"Aviella!" I cry out, following her out in time to see her body drop back and her head crack against the wall behind her.

I scoop her limp form up into my arms and flow healing magic into her body. It won't help much, but it will heal any damage from her head hitting the wall. Her eyes flutter, then open. She shakes her head and sits up, not pulling out of my arms.

"That was tough," she says.

"Yes," I agree. "I pushed you hard. We have to be prepared."

"It's good," she says, her eyelids dropping to half, head tilting back.

I'm acutely aware of her body in my arms, pressing against mine. The beauty of her face is akin to the Divine, a study that I could undertake forever. The fullness of her lips calls me, begging me to taste them. My cock stiffens as desire rages through my veins.

It's not time. I can't, no matter how much I want to, this isn't the moment. I don't know when that moment will be, I only hope it is soon. I have enough free will that I could act. I could join with her, give in to the lustful feelings, but if I do it will be bad. Bad in ways I don't know or understand. It's an instinct, a knowingness that I could never put into words.

She pushes closer, her breasts crushing against my chest. I lean in, her lips becoming my sole focus. I have to taste them, knowing they will be as sweet as the finest wine. Her magic caresses my skin with light touches. My own Divine magic rises to its call, entwining with it as I want my body to entwine with hers.

It's easy. Less than an inch, our lips will touch, and I will give myself to her as she offers herself to me. The temptation of her is an intoxicating rarity. I'm dancing on the edge between desire and reason. My cock pounds, blood rushes in my ears, heart racing. Her breath brushes my lips I'm so close, her eyes closed, her arms encircling me.

No!

Drawing my magic back, I change the angle of my head and place a single, gentle kiss on her forehead. An empty ache fills my core as my cock and body rages against the control. Her eyes open. Her jaw drops in surprise. I pull back and rise from the bed, putting what little space between us that I can.

"We should shower," I say.

"Oh," she says, her eyelids dropping again and a seductive smile playing on her lips.

"Separately," I say, sterner than I intend.

My blood is running too hot, my emotions are high, it's all I can do to remain in control.

"Right," she says, her cheeks flushing soft pink.

Regret is an empty pit in my stomach. I turn and exit the too-small space, already regretting my decision even though I know with certainty it was the right one.

CHAPTER SIX

AVIELLA

J'm light-headed to the point of being almost dizzy watching him leave my room. Magic buzzes, rumbling deep inside, accenting and toying with the base desire. Taking a deep breath, I close my eyes and hold it. I know, for certain, that Nathanial is one of mine. We're meant to be together.

Each time I join with one of the guys, it unlocks more of my power. It's scary, exciting, and overwhelming. At this point, though, I'll do whatever I have to do to win. And winning means saving my Dad. After that, I'm going to find the Big Bad, whoever or whatever it is, and I'm going to kick its ass. Or I'm going to try.

I climb to my feet and grab the wall to steady myself. Nathanial's magic swirls through, combines with my own, and intertwines with my desire. When I breathe slowly, the room stops spinning, and I'm oriented back in the here and now.

Outside the door, Nate is waiting, arms crossed and face stoic, but I don't miss the way his eyes drink me in. My body warms, butterflies dance in my stomach, and I want him.

More importantly, he wants me. He may be playing hard to get, but there is no doubt of his desire. The weight of his gaze tells me all I need to know.

Smiling I silently brush against him as I pass, teasingly. He bites his lip, stiffening as I move beyond him, then follows me down the small hall to the shower. I stop in the door and turn to face him. Our eyes lock together, and it feels as if part of the universe clicks into place.

"Guess I'll shower," I say, and bite my lip.

Magic surges, pulsing and reaching out to caress him. I can't stop it, I don't have that much control. His jaw tightens, but it's the only outward sign he gives me.

"Good," he says, barely opening his mouth.

I linger in the door waiting to see if he's going to give in to desire, but he doesn't move. At last I step inside alone. The lukewarm water rinses away the sweat from training. I lather myself, but as I move the rough, homemade bar of soap over my breasts, it passes across my sensitive nipples and I gasp.

Sensation explodes, rocking my world. I hadn't noticed how hard my nipples were. The roughness of the soap fills my thoughts with memories of rough tongues working on each of my breasts while another, hot and ready mouth worked my mound.

I'm groaning. The memories of joining with the dragons dance through my thoughts, and my body responds in kind. Instinctively I grab one breast and squeeze, while my hand holding the soap moves lower, over my hips to soap my ass. I run the rough bar between my cheeks, teasing the secretive hole while stretching my fingers out to caress my pussy.

I have to bite my lips to lock in a moan. Nate's teasing me. I want him. No, I need him. Moving the soap around to my front I lather up, covering myself with a nice layer before putting the bar back on the tiny shelf. The water is getting cooler, if I don't hurry there won't be any warm water for him.

Serves him right.

Cupping my mound with my right hand I work my tits with my left. The nipples are so sensitive each pass over them is almost too much. I'm fighting to not cry out, but the pleasure keeps building. Pressing harder and rubbing my hooded clit I build myself up to a fast and hard orgasm.

He wants me. The dragon magic surges up, co-mingling with my own. Tynan's magic is dominance, control. It pushes me to take charge, and so I do. I own my needs, and if Nate isn't going to fulfill them, I will. Here and now.

"Mmmm," it slips out before I can stop it.

Fuck, this feels so good. The memories call back the sensations of taking the three dragons. Before, I would have considered myself bad, or naughty, or worse things for having done that, but not anymore. I'm empowered. They empowered me.

There is no mistaking it. I didn't get used, I used them. I took power from each of them with my sex. They became mine the same way I'm going to make Nate mine. And Rafe, and Efram, even stoic Silas. They're my men. My protectors, my friends, but more: my lovers. I'm not wrong for having them. We're meant to be.

I'm right. I'm the Chosen One. I didn't choose to be, but I am. The sooner I accept my role, my purpose in life the sooner I'll become what I'm supposed to. Soon... I'm so close. It's building, a crescendo of power, peaking with each one I join.

Almost there.

Pleasure explodes, forcing me to lean against the wall, panting. The water turns cold. I've taken too long. I push off the wall, but find I have to use it to keep myself up—my knees are still weak from the orgasm. Once the final wave passes, I let out a long exhale, then rinse off.

Wrapping a towel around myself, I walk out the door to find Nate waiting.

"All yours," I smile, cheeks warming as I stare into his steady gaze.

"Thank you," he says, holding himself stiffly.

Feeling particularly bold, I walk closer and rest my fingers on the stubble of his cheek. Magic flares at the touch. He leans into my touch, head tilting down, eyes closing, and his lips parting.

"Soon," I whisper, then turn and walk away.

I can feel his eyes on me until I move out of sight and into my own room. I use the towel to dry my hair then pull on a loose t-shirt and the least ragged jeans I own. The sound of the train is the only comfort in the empty room. Hmm, coffee. Everything is better with coffee, and Tynan made sure the train is well stocked.

Dressed and hair at least finger styled, I go to the dining area and set about brewing coffee. None of the boys are around, each off doing their own thing, but I really don't want to be alone. I wonder what Silas is doing so I pour two cups of coffee and go in search of him.

It can't be that hard to find him—the train is limited in space after all. I'm right in that it doesn't take long to find him tucked into a corner reading a book. He barely glances up as I make my way through the stocks to join him. When I hold out the cup of coffee, he takes it, thanking me absently but never taking his attention fully off the book.

I take a seat on a box opposite him and sip my coffee, waiting for him to finish what he's doing. At last he looks up, places a finger in the book, and closes it with delicate care. He sips the coffee and murmurs another thanks.

"Of course," I say, raising my cup to him before taking another sip.

His eyes look me over with cold calculation and evaluation. In any other man it would bother me, but Silas is Silas. His face softens as he nods and drinks more coffee.

"Your assimilating the power well," he says.

"Thanks?" I ask more than say.

I'm not sure if that's a compliment or a backhanded stab. He grunts in response, adding no clarity to the comment. I decide to take it in stride. What am I going to do, argue with him? Tynan's and his brothers' magic was almost too much, and it has been difficult to get it under control.

"Give it to me straight," I say, changing the subject. "How bad is the Mega-church?"

He looks thoughtful, sips the coffee, then a soft smile plays on his lips.

"Batshit crazy. Raving mad," he says. I snort the coffee I was trying to sip at his unexpected response. His slight smile becomes a rare full grin. "We'll make it through. Between us we have contacts and some allies inside. We can keep you safe."

"Is this a good idea then?" I ask.

He shrugs and shakes his head. "We don't have many options, do we?"

"No," I agree, frowning. "Is there one leader? How does this place operate?"

"It's like a televangelist's dream gone to extreme," he says. "Frederick Jones is charismatic, charming, and as sick and twisted as they come. Before the Apocalypse he was a minor circuit preacher, moving from tent revival to tent revival subsiding on the fringes of society and religious belief.

"After... he came into his own. His followers are fanatics of the most extreme degree. He preaches of cleansing the flesh in order to purify the soul. That there is little time left to repent, for most, it is already too late."

"Sounds like a charmer," I say.

"Actually," Silas says. "He is. Incredibly so. His power is magnetic. I suspect he has latent magic talents that he would never be able to develop, because if he did then he'd be betraying his own preaching."

"He doesn't like magic?" I ask.

"Magic is of the devil," Silas says. "Or so he preaches. It should be cleansed from the flesh."

"Cleansed?" I ask.

"Yes," Silas nods.

"I don't suppose he means a nice hot bath with some soap?"

"You assume correctly," Silas says.

"Great," I say. "Why are we going here again?"

"Because there are Innocents here and because it's the next most likely place to find your father," he says.

"Right," I say, finishing off my coffee. "Great. Well, this ought to be a good time."

Silas grunts and opens his book, returning his attention to it. I sit in silence contemplating my own future and mortality. How do I save a world that doesn't seem to want to be saved?

CHAPTER SEVEN

AVIELLA

his is the longest journey ever. It brings back memories of traveling with my Dad from before the Fall. Hours spend cuddled up in blankets leaning my head against the door of whatever car he'd managed to acquire. I'd watch the scenery rolling past.

It was all normal to me. I never really considered that other people didn't live like we did. On the run, separate from everyone else. The two of us against the world. His warm baritone voice echoes in my memory while I lay in my bed debating whether or not I want to get up.

"You're special, Aviella," he said, smiling as he glances over.

"Why, Daddy?" I ask.

"Because of your Mommy," he says. "You aren't only her gift to me, you're her gift to the world."

Normal. It all seemed normal. What father doesn't dote on his daughter? I never took it seriously, not back then. I was loved and he always talked of my mother, but she was barely a memory for me. Still all I remember is dim images of a bright face outlined in sunshine and light. She was gone before I formed any lasting impression more than warmth and love.

I know she loved me. I don't understand where she went —Dad never told me—but she's also never been my focus. Dad was there, always, until he wasn't. Now I know, though, I have to save him. It's on me. Me and my new friends. What will he think of them?

I think he'd like Rafe, actually. Chuckling I imagine the two of them meeting. Rafe's easy going attitude and the way he refuses to take anything too serious. Dad would either love him or hate him. Efram he would like for sure. He's definitely the kind of man Dad would approve of. Silas is iffy, and Nate would be okay sure. Tynan... no that's the kind of man he would warn me away from.

Dangerous, controlling, a little dark, but damn if he isn't sexy as hell with the way he dominates any scene he walks into. Even with his brothers, alpha extremes in their own right, he stands above.

"I'm coming, Daddy," I repeat the mantra.

It's my stable point. The one thing I can cling to, that I'm certain of in a world of uncertainty. Forces array against us—no, against me. I guess Daddy was right, I'm special. I still don't know how to accept this or what it means, but there can be no doubt that everywhere I go, trouble follows.

Something itches at the edges of my thoughts, like I've forgotten something important. I try to figure it out, but every time I almost have it the concept flitters away. The window draws my attention. Something outside? Did I miss something?

Sitting partway up I look out the window, but nothing stands out. The blasted landscape rolls by, which is pretty much the usual. No monsters in sight, nothing that grabs my attention. Weird. Sighing, I roll out of bed and stretch. I put on the cleanest clothes I can find, walk out, and immediately smell coffee.

In the kitchen area, everyone is gathered, and breakfast is being served. It's all freeze-dried nutri-meals, but food is food. I've never been picky which serves you well during the Apocalypse. Maybe that's my superpower.

"We shouldn't go through there again," Nate says.

"I agree," Rafe says, placing a plate of the nutri-equivalent of pancakes on the table.

"It's the most direct route," Silas says.

"Go through where?" I ask.

"Wormwood," Efram says.

Tingles like someone is walking across my grave run down my back, and I suppress a shiver. Even the name of the place is enough to make me afraid. We survived part of it, but the heart of it was… bad.

"Do we have a choice?" I ask. "We're not in control of the train, are we?"

"There is a track change ahead," Nate says. "We could redirect and go around it."

"But it would be monumentally stupid," Silas says.

"I disagree," Rafe says.

"I don't," Efram says. "Time is running out, we need to get to New Jerusalem."

New Jerusalem, the next mega-bunker on our journey. Where the crazies go, home of the New World church. Or the mockery of what a church should be, at least.

"Why didn't you guys bring this up last night?" I ask, irritation chasing away the hints of fear.

Magic rises tingling my skin and making the air all but crackle as it becomes charged with the potential energy. Nate and Efram exchange a look while Rafe looks away from me. Silas alone stoically meets my gaze but doesn't answer.

"Well?" I ask, challenging all of them to answer me.

"There could be trouble," Rafe says.

"What else is new?" I ask, shrugging. "Trouble follows us. Hell, we could be the storm bringers. Look at the mess we've left in our wake!"

"And would you counsel that we go into a stronghold of the enemy then?" Silas asks, his eyes judging my every word and motion.

I'm almost overwhelmed with an urge to make him proud, to say or do the right thing. I want his approval. It's ridiculous, I'm not a little girl or in need of his approval for anything.

"I don't know," I flash off angrily. "I'm not sure I have all the data to think with, since you guys seem to want to make a habit of keeping me out of the loop."

I curse myself for feeling a tingle of delight at the approving smile that plays across Silas's face. Damn him, this is his fault too.

"Aviella, you've been on edge," Efram says. "Don't take it personally. We didn't see the need to worry you with things that don't matter."

"Things that don't matter?" I ask, voice dropping lower.

The dragon magic swirls through me, threatening my control. It doesn't matter if I understand what they were trying to do, logically. Their actions act against my dominance. Hiding things from me isn't the way of a dragon. A dragon would punish them.

I'm not a dragon. I'm a woman, I'm me. As I fight the swirling urges brought on by Tynan's magic they watch. Each of them is doing what they think is best, and I know it. There is no doubt in my mind, but that does nothing to lessen my irritation.

"Or we could be a bunch of over-protective idiots, each of us doing our best to care for you," Rafe says, grinning.

His wild-magic caresses my skin, pushing into and

mingling with my magic as it does. The lightness of his touch breaks through my anger.

"Right," I sigh. "Look, we're in this together. No more secrets. I mean it, if you know something, we all need to know it. Got it?"

The men exchange looks with each other before nodding their assent. Somehow, I doubt this will be the last time they hold anything back. There's nothing I can do about it though, and that leaves me antsy and irritable.

"Coffee?" Rafe asks, holding up the pot.

"Please," I say. He pours a cup and hands it over. Curling my fingers around the warm cup helps. "So what are the ramifications of our choice?"

"If we go around, the journey is going to take longer, possibly a week, maybe a little less depending on what we run into," Silas says.

"That's bad?" I ask.

"The longer we are outside the protection of a bunker, the more exposed we are," Silas says. "Hence cutting through the Wormwood territory is the best option."

"But Wormwood is bad," I observe, making it an understatement on purpose.

"Bad is relative," Rafe laughs. "Take yours truly."

I roll my eyes at the demon.

"Yes," Silas agrees. "It's dangerous, more dangerous than ever, but I don't believe it compares to running into a trumpet beast. Or the fact that out here, in the open, we are exposed to a direct attack with little to no repercussions. This could be an end-game move."

"Shit," I exhale.

The coffee is weak, watery, but still delicious and soothing. Since the Fall, luxury has taken on an entirely new meaning. No one says anything for a several seconds while we eat and contemplate the options.

"The clues to my Father lie in New Jerusalem," I state. "The faster we get there, the faster we save him."

"Aviella," Nate says. He drags my name out and it's obvious he's choosing his words carefully. "We might already be… too late."

"No," I disagree.

"You can't be—" he starts

"I am," I cut him off.

"Avi, it could be a trap," Rafe says. "Trust me, I know what I'm talking about here."

"I do trust you," I say, rising to my feet. "I trust all of you but in this matter, you have to trust me. I *know* I'm right."

There's another long moment as they look to each other, but no one wants to argue with me. Or if they do, they swallow it, which is fine with me. I'm not in the mood for this.

"We're going through it," I order, rising to my feet.

"Very well," Silas says.

I wait, looking around the table until I'm sure no one wants to offer anymore argument. Satisfied that the decision is made, I take my coffee and walk out of the car.

The air outside as I move between the cars has a sulfur tang to it. There's no doubt we're close to Wormwood. That scent is unmistakable. I can't put my attention on that right now, but I need something to focus on. The hair on the back of my neck itches. Stopping before I enter the next car I look up and around. It feels like I'm being watched, but I can't see anything that would make me feel that way.

Weird.

Shaking it off I go into the car ahead. The refugees are having their breakfast. The buzz of conversation stops when I enter and their gazes turn to me. The empty eyes, blank faces, and the overall sense of their despair hits me like walking into a heavy fog.

Closing my eyes for a moment I drink it in, and god help me, it feels invigorating to take in their losses. It feels dirty and weird, but no matter all that the tingling sensation in my core is delightful. I stop at one young couple and kneel in front of them. They would be considered beautiful if they were well-fed, but now they're thin to the point of being gaunt. It's sad.

"How are you?" I ask.

The girl brightens, a smile flashing.

"We're good. How could we not be?" She straightens her back and leans in close. "Have you seen Sarah? She's such a shit-show. Tynan will never notice her."

She glances over my shoulder, her smile widening.

"Oh," I say, my own hope being dashed.

They haven't changed. They're still vying for his attention. I rise to my feet and turn my back on her. The pettiness turns my stomach. I'd intended to spend some time with the survivors and see if I could help, but bile rises in my throat. My stomach is churning, and as I look around the car, it hits me. They're all the same. None of them are going to change easily. They don't know any other life.

The weight of it settles on my shoulders and I turn away, heading for my room. This wasn't a good idea after all.

CHAPTER EIGHT

EFRAM

*P*ain stabs into my head, sharp and fast as a scream echoes through the ether. My magic surges, causing the pathways to tingle and itch. Something has happened.

I rise from the table, ignore the continuing conversation, and follow the sense of wrongness. Someone has died and it wasn't peaceful. None of the others pay attention to my leaving. My place in this group is always that of an outsider anyway. What am I doing here?

I'm a necroseer. The least of any magic user from before the Fall, and after? At least before I had a good job and a reason to be useful. There were people who cared about wrongful deaths. There was at least some form of justice. What is there to be offered now?

No, my place isn't well set here among the power houses that Aviella has gathered. On a scale of power, I'm the lowest, but I hope that on a scale of friendship, I'm the highest. Or something like that. It's hard to think about. I'm the outsider so often, and at times it seems I'm living off the scraps of her attention. It's not her fault in any way.

These men that are drawn to her are powerful beings, dominant. They take center stage by their very presence. That's not me, never has been, and especially not since I lost my sister. No, I've always been most comfortable out of the spotlight. Even now, when I see how she glows and watching her grow as she gathers us around her…. it's all I need.

It's more than enough. I'm happy to be one of her disciples. What an odd thought. The sound of someone crying cuts through my introspection. I slide my way through the overcrowded cars and stop in front of a sobbing man. He has his head in his hands and doesn't look up. I tap his shoulder until at last he does, tears streaming down his face.

"What is it?" I ask.

"She's gone," he says, sobs cutting off any further response.

"Who is?" I ask, kneeling in front of him.

Dozens of eyes watch. Any one of them could be a perpetrator. In this world, where these people came from, it could be the man in front of me. I won't know until I find the body of the spirit that cried out for justice.

"Abigail," he sobs. "I can't find her."

I want to offer him some comfort, but I've got nothing to give. There is no doubt in my mind that she's dead. All I can offer any of them now is justice. Justice in a world gone wrong. It won't set anything right, nothing that matters anyway. He'll be alone.

I turn my back on him and walk ahead, pulled by my magic. It takes a while. The murderer was clever in their crime. The body is tucked away in a storage car that is too full for any refugees to try and make a space in. When I climb over a stack of crates, I find her.

She was pretty, once. She has the gauntness that was popular in Tynan's bunker, especially among those vying for the status of a 'darling'. Her glassy eyes stare up at me. Her mouth hangs open. I squeeze into the tight space with her until I'm close enough to see the finger marks on her neck. Strangulation.

Someone on the train is a murderer. On the train with Aviella. Justice or no, changing the world or not, I can't let a murderer be this close to Aviella. No matter why this person did it, once they've crossed that line they've gone too far.

Resting my fingertips on the bodies forehead I will my magic into it, calling her back, pulling her from the swirling ether where she's trapped herself, unwilling to move on without some finality. Her eyes clear, mouth snaps shut, then she screams.

"Stop that," I order, pushing magic and enforcing my command.

Her teeth clack, she shuts her jaw so hard and fast. Tears well in her eyes and she trembles but doesn't make any noise. My magic restrains her.

"There isn't much time," I say. "Who did this to you?"

The trembling increases until she's almost spasming. I ease back my magic and she sobs, gasping in unnecessary air.

"Oh god," she cries. "Her hands, they're on my throat. She won't let go!"

"I know," I say, speaking softly, the ache in my heart almost too much to bear. My magic, my job has never been an easy one. "Who? Who is it?"

"Brenda," she gasps, the light in her eyes fading as her soul gives up its final burden. "Brenda…"

Her voice echoes as if coming to me down a long tunnel, and her eyes become dull and lifeless. I close her eyes and send up a prayer that she find her rest. No one deserves a death like this. It doesn't matter though, her fate isn't the worst, in a lot of ways it might be the easiest. Easier than most of us are likely to find.

As I climb back to the path, I debate how to handle the

next part. We can't allow this on the train. It's too dangerous. Any of the passengers giving into their darkest desires and impulses opens a door to the Shadow. That puts Aviella at risk, and that is one thing I can't allow.

The only question is, really, do I tell her? She's already on edge and struggling to control her growing powers. I can't honestly tell what her reaction would be. She could lose it, if she can't stay on top of the dragon magic pushing her. It could go a hundred different ways, none of them good. No, it's best if she's not involved, no matter how much she hates it when we hide things from her. Keeping her focused on training and improving her control is a better use of her time and energy. This isn't a matter for her.

No, the man for this job is Rafe. The demon will be able to sense out this Brenda easier than any of us. Her darkness will call to him, and he's most uniquely suited for doing what is necessary after that. Decision made, I go to find him, and avoid running into Aviella first.

CHAPTER NINE

RAFE

"Tell me," I say, soothingly. "Why did she have to go?"

Brenda smiles, the devil in her eyes and in her grin. And I know, better than anyone, what that looks like. She almost laughs, the delight on her face beaming.

"Because she was the competition," she says, enthusiastically waving her arms. "She had those cheekbones, god I'd kill to have her cheekbones. Well, I guess I did."

She confides in me easily. I let my magic caress across her, easing her reservations, pulling the darkness out of its hiding recesses. She's so proud it's almost too easy. Efram is tense standing behind me. His frustration and irritation is palpable.

"Efram, if you can't control it, leave," I say without looking at him. He grunts in response but doesn't leave. "You did, didn't you? Tell me more."

"You get it, don't you?" she asks, leaning in conspiratorially. "You've done bad things too. I know it was bad, but I had to. I didn't have a choice, don't you see? I have to be best. If I'm not best, then what am I?"

"What are we all if we're not best?" I ask and Efram harrumphs.

"Right? I mean what else is there? The entire world has gone to hell. The best get what they want. They have the nice things. They get to eat! They don't have to..."

She trails off the darkness clouding her eyes, but in that darkness, I see her pain. The memories of things she's done are far outweighed by the things done to her. No one is born like this, they're made. She's a victim of circumstance as much as the criminal. Which came first? The crime or the criminal?

A philosophical question for the ages.

"Tell me," I say.

Her pain is raw, heavy and real. It calls to me and my magic pulls it out of her. Behind the pain is despair and that is a heady delight. The emptiness in the core of what would be my soul hungers for it. I want to feast on it, gorge myself without consideration of the consequences. Restraint is the better than desire, so I hold back.

"It's not my fault," she says, tears welling in her eyes and for the first time I see regret. "She wouldn't back down. I had to, don't you see? You understand, right?"

"Of course I do," I say, touching her cheek and trailing my fingers down her jawline.

She smiles, certainty filling her eyes. The touch strengthens my connection to her, and I see what I feared most. Tendrils of the Shadow. She's opened her soul to it with her heinous act. It's exactly what Efram was afraid of, the most dangerous thing. The Shadow is recruiting and isn't circumspect about who or when. We're in a war after all.

"One way or another, she had to go," she says. "If I'm the best, then he'll shine his favor on me. They'll all regret it then. They'll see I'm worth something. I'm not trash, not a loser, like the rest of them. He'll find me and take me to his suites."

She's almost delusional. It's as if she doesn't even know that Tynan's entire bunker has been destroyed, lost to the forces of darkness.

"What else could a girl want?" I purr.

"Exactly! There's nothing else that matters. I'll be the best, I'll eat the best food, have the best dresses, I'll be the Queen!"

"We need to get this over with," Efram hisses behind me. "Quit playing with her."

"My friend," I say. "I am not 'playing' with her. Let me do my work."

He shifts restlessly but doesn't interfere further. I could end this now, but I don't want to, if only to not appear to be doing so on his command. That's childish, I know it, but I've never claimed to be more than a petty demon after all.

"I'm so glad I met you," Brenda smiles broadly, beaming. "You get it. None of those others, they don't understand. All I've done, it's finally going to pay off. You're going to help, aren't you? I feel it in you, we're the same you and I. He'll take you too, you know? Tynan isn't picky about things like that. You could be the King to my Queen. Well, he's the King of course, but you could be a Duke!"

"That sounds delightful," I say.

Pushing magic into her I pull the strings of her carnal desires. This doesn't have to be unpleasant and she's been through enough. Doing what is necessary doesn't have to be mean. Her lips part, pink tongue licking them, and her eyes burn with lust. She leans towards me, her hands reaching instinctively out.

Leaning in I take her lips, and when she has given herself over to the pleasures, my magic ignites. I pull, drawing the darkness off her. She struggles, fighting what's happening, but she can't stop. All the pain, the despair, I take off of her soul and then, once I've feasted on it all, I pull her out and set her free.

Her body slumps and her eyes grow lifeless. She'll find her rest in the other realms, once she's been weighed and judged, but I've done what I can for her. The pain and despair I've taken off of her will lessen any time she has to spend in Purgatory.

Efram turns around and stares. There's a strange mix of awe and anger in his face. His tense jaw, his hard eyes stare, but he doesn't say anything. I understand. What I do isn't pleasant, and in any other circumstances I wouldn't have allowed him to witness it.

"It's over," I say.

"Yeah," he says. "Why?"

"Why?" I ask, frowning.

"Why did you lighten her load? She murdered that girl."

"She did," I agree, crossing my arms over my chest.

"So why lighten her load? Let her pay the price when she reaches the other side."

"What good would that do?" I ask, shaking my head. "She's as much victim as the girl she killed. They all are."

"Victim!" he says.

"Yes," I say, unperturbed by his sudden outburst.

His magic crackles but he knows he's no match for me. It's not even enough of a challenge to trigger my instincts.

"How do you think she's a victim?" he asks.

"She wanted to be better, to have better things, to have power," I say. "She bought into the bill of goods."

"Sure, they all have, that doesn't lessen her sins," he says.

"Doesn't it? An entire society dedicated to a twisted desire for things. She was raised in it, grooved into it. What choices did she have at any point along the way? What guiding light was there for her?"

His face softens, but he's still tense.

"Sure, but that doesn't make what she did right," he says.

"No, it doesn't, but it does make her understandable. She'll serve her time, her soul will be weighed, she'll be judged and found wanting," I say.

"But it won't be as bad?" he asks.

"No, it won't," I say, glancing at her. "We need to do something with this or Aviella will find out."

I change the subject, done with this conversation. I'm a demon, I've done so much worse than Brenda, but I've always done it for good reasons. Or at least reasons that seemed good to me. She grew up in a dark and twisted world before the Apocalypse, and it has only been made worse by the loss of the good ones who went with the Rapture.

A society that worshipped possessions. Constantly sold to the populace in bright moving pictures showing how great your life could be. Social media where everyone filters out the negative and falsely cast their lives into a make-believe perfection. Drugs that make everything okay, chemically, but not a single consideration given to the spiritual.

No, she made her choices and she'll pay for them, but it doesn't need to be as bad as it can be. I saved her from that at least. It's the only comfort I find in what I am.

CHAPTER TEN

SILAS

*N*othing in my long existence has been harder than not letting myself indulge in Aviella. Her spirit is pure, the purest thing I've ever known. I've swam, energetically, through her blood and the potential she has is off the charts.

She's intoxicating. Enticing, pulling me in, creating a desire to throw caution to the wind. It's not who I am. My life has been one of careful consideration. Desire isn't new, I've known it before but with her it's almost as if it is a different thing too.

My fingers drift over the papyrus pages of the book I'm reading. The printed words flow in more than I read them as a mortal would. Knowledge, in any form, is meant to be known. There are no secrets in the world for those who are willing to look, but more importantly, willing to know. The majority live their lives in self-delusion and denial. They create the boundaries of what they believe to be, and that then becomes the cage that entraps them. A prison of their own ideals.

That lie was one of the first that set me on my path. Even

the concepts of life and death are constructs, agreed on so they became so. I never agreed to them, so I live. I continue in my relentless pursuit of knowledge.

Hmm, this is of interest. Aviella's blood line traces back through the passage of time to ancient ancestors, but along the way it was mingled with others. This book gives me new insight into something I detected but didn't understand, some of her genetics comes from an ancient enclave of sorcerers in what modern historians would call Persia.

The old man of the mountain was a late comer to this game, depending on the use of drugs and mind control much more than true magic but he is of the same blood, though his magic was weak in comparison to his and Aviella's ancestors. Interesting, it's a balance to what I've found in her.

Her innate sense of justice will either be her saving grace or her downfall. If she falls, we all fall, so maybe knowing something of this will help her. I absorb the rest of the information before deciding to go and see her.

It's a risk. When she was last in here it took all my composure to resist her advances. Still, it is my duty to empower her, to guide her and keep her looking forward. Giving her knowledge is the greatest good, for all of us. Decision made, I leave the small room and make my way through the train.

When I pass a window, the hair on the back of my neck stands on end. Something is off…

The window seems fine, the wards are intact, and nothing outside catches my attention. I watch for several minutes but the sensation doesn't return. I file it away as something to be aware of but for now there is nothing I can do with an unknown. As I turn from the window Rafe's magic surges behind me, brief and quick, but distinctive to the demon. I'll follow up with him on what happened later, but there's no alarm so I'm not going to worry about it now.

"Hey," Aviella says, stopping the motion she was in the middle of.

She's practicing the battle stances that Nathanial has been teaching her. Pride wells in my chest. She is by far the best student I've ever taken under my wing. I would give anything to protect her from what we face.

"Hello," I say, "don't let me interrupt."

"It's fine," she smiles, arms dropping to her side. "I'm antsy, passing the time with some practice. What's up?"

A light sheen of sweat accents her natural beauty. Her unkempt hair forming a halo around her angelic face, her chest rising and falling with heavy breathing, pushing her breasts tight against the cloth of her shirt. Her nipples are erect, poking through the fabric. My cock stiffens, reacting to the burning passion in my soul. Swallowing, I push it aside. Now is not the time.

"I've learned more of your ancestry," I say. "I thought you'd like to know."

"Oh, cool," she says, moving closer.

Gods help me, my breath catches in my chest as she comes closer. Her hand reaches towards me and my cock rages, ready to be released, my heart races, pulse pounding in my ears. Her hand moves past me and grabs a towel. She dries her face but remains standing inches in front of me.

It's nothing. She means nothing by it, there's little space on the crowded and well-stocked train cars. That's all it is. Or so I keep telling myself.

She inhales and I'm acutely aware of the way her breasts brush against my chest. Her eyes smolder with offered desire. Temptation is a cruel mistress. She bites her lower lip and I barely stop myself from bending in and kissing her.

"Some of your ancestors," I say, forcing myself to focus, "were powerful sorcerers. They dealt with gray magic."

"Gray?" she asks.

"Yes," I say. She frowns, her brow furrowing. She steps away and air returns to the room as she turns her mind to understanding. "Gray," I continue. "There exists a theory that there are gradations of magic. Magic is intention, as I've taught you, but Alexitar theorized that even so, there are degrees of the purity of magic. He represented this by colors."

"Let me guess, white to black?" she asks.

"Exactly, with gradations in between," I say.

"So gray," she says, nodding her understanding. "Nathanial would be white, Rafe black, and then there's everything that falls between."

"More or less, yes," I agree. "It would come down to the service and intention the magic was being put to. Did it help more of life than it harmed? What degree, if you will, did it go to make things better?"

"Okay," she says, running her fingers through her hair and pulling out tangles.

My hands itch with desire for it to be my fingers running through her hair. My lips tingle with the need to taste her.

"We know your bloodline is powerful, but finding this connection helps me understand," I say.

"Understand what?" she asks, stopping what she's doing and focusing on me with curiosity.

"You," I say, the word catching in my throat.

"Me?" she asks, doubt in her eyes. "What about me?"

"You're... impossible," I admit. "You master different types of magic, which is difficult at the very least. It takes years of dedicated study, but you do it easily. In days at the most. Nate's magic, Rafe's, Efram's too if I'm not mistaken."

She nods her agreement. "And Tynan's."

"Tynan's most of all," I agree.

She purses her lips and resumes fingering out her hair. "Okay, so what about it?"

"Your ancestry is unique," I say.

"So?" she asks.

"The odds against the exact combination that makes up your body are.... Astronomical. It lends itself to the idea of its being intended. Guided. If so..."

"Wait, what are you saying?" she asks.

"What do you recall of your mother?" I ask.

She frowns deeply. "Not much. Light, a pretty face, her voice mostly. Her voice was soothing but aren't all mom's voices soothing?"

"I see," I say.

"See what, Silas?" she asks. Finished with her hair, she moves closer.

Her hips sway, her chest rises and falls, her full lips purse. My resolve is crumbling. She is irresistible.

"I don't know, yet," I say. "It seems very possible that you were... intended. To be here, at this time, with this body."

"This body?" she asks, her voice thick with her own lust and desire.

Her magic caresses my skin, calling to my own. It's the softest touch of a gentle lover, waking one from sleep. Calling you from the realms of sleep to welcome you into their arms. Caution dies in a scream as she hooks her fingers into my belt loop, pulling me close.

I take her lips. Rougher than I intend, desire tossing aside care and consideration. She responds in kind. Her arms wrap around my neck, jerking me even closer.

She thrusts her hips into me, and my hard cock is crushed between us. When I take her in my arms, relief and tension happen together. She wraps her legs around my waist, wiggling herself against me. She moans into our kiss, adjusting herself until my cock is pushing hard against the clothing blocking her opening from me.

I twine my hands in her hair, pull her head back, and

expose her neck. Kiss my way down her soft skin to her shoulder. She grinds against me and my cock throbs with need.

I turn to pin her against the wall, freeing my hands to roam down her body, under her shirt. Her feverish skin welcomes my touch. She gasps as I slide my hands up and find her breasts. Soft, repeating moans as I dry thrust against her while working her nipples.

Each thrust up is the sweetest torture. I grab her shirt, pull it over her head, and toss it aside. Angling back, I admire, once again, the perfect swell of her breasts. The hard nipples so erect they look painful. She smiles, her eyes half-lidded, then pushes her hands between us and under the fabric of my pants.

Her touch on my cock makes me gasp, and it spasms in relief at her attention. Her delicate fingers tease the head as they pass over it and wrap around the shaft. She strokes, slowly, so slowly it's painful.

Her magic passes over me like the waves of an ocean, and while we delicately explore each other's bodies, the joining on the metaphysical realm is the crashing together of two storms. Experiencing the sensations on both levels, polar opposites, is overwhelming.

She's a raging hurricane, her magic the equivalent of tsunami class waves crashing into me. Wearing down my barriers.

My own magic rages, against yet yearning for hers. She's wild, free, controlled but only in the barest way. She lets the magic carry her, whereas I keep mine tight. Exacting.

I want to let it go. To join her, to become a storm the likes of which this world has never seen.

Through her magic I see the others that she's joined to her. Their magic swirls and augments hers, but hers alone is the binding thread. Pulling our disparate mob into a cohesive whole.

She rips my shirt open, kissing my neck. I kiss her bare shoulder then hook my hands under her ass and carry her to the bed.

I lay her on it and roughly pull off her pants. It's time. I have to be inside of her now.

Her magic is penetrating my barriers, and I need to penetrate her flesh before I completely lose control. She tears at the binding of my own pants, and they give way before her onslaught of attention.

My cock drops free, swollen purple with need. She grabs it with one hand, not being gentle, pulling me into her.

As I penetrate her flesh, the warm wetness welcoming me home, the storm of her magic breaks through the last of my barriers.

Our magic swirls together as our bodies join into one. There's no holding back, we're riding the edge the moment we start. Her cries of pleasure with each thrust match my own.

My magic pushes against hers and she takes it all. Takes my cock, takes my magic; she absorbs them, claims them as she makes it all a part of her. She is all, she is more, the key that unlocks us. It is she who makes us more, and she alone who gives us a chance against that which we face.

Our bodies rise and fall from each other as our magic swells the raging storm until both as one explode. The pleasures of the flesh are but pale echoes of the creation happening on the higher realms. The raging storm of magic calms without losing its rage.

We collapse onto the bed, panting as we recover from our spent energies. Rolling off of her I lie to one side and she rests her head on my shoulder.

"Good?" she asks, and I laugh.

"Isn't that my role to ask?" I respond, and she laughs.

Laying an arm over her shoulders I close my eyes for a moment and cherish this brief respite. If only I could keep her like this. Safe. Protected. In my arms.

I don't mind sharing her with the others, but I don't want to share her with the world. I know what this world can do. What it will do. I don't know that we, even all of us together, can protect her. It's very likely we'll lose, lose her, lose everything.

That sobering thought destroys the afterglow.

CHAPTER ELEVEN

AVIELLA

*P*ower courses through my veins. It's almost as if hidden doors unlock as I look around my own thoughts. Things I've known? No, things he's known or knows. Books he's read. Stories, histories. Innumerable writs, scrolls, even clay tablets of hidden knowledge.

How much has he read? It's as if I've gained access to his memories, but not all of them. Only things he's read. Weird.

It's probably not that. That really doesn't make much sense but maybe it does? Who knows? Right now I feel great. My body is satisfied and more, my magic is sated. Sometimes it seems to have a hunger and need of its own. I'm not sure if it's my magic, my fate, or self-delusion that has set me barreling along this path, but whatever it is, we're in it together.

That brings me a degree of comfort I don't know how else I would find. Can I know what he's read, really? Is this some construct my mind is creating to give definition to my own magic, or is it real? What does Silas read for pleasure?

That's an interesting question. I know he's a voracious reader, but all I ever see him reading is texts on magic, history, genealogies, boring stuff. What does he read to escape?

Can I?

When I reach out with my magic, it feels like I can know this. I'm not sure how, but I will myself to know, basic guiding of magic 101. Something pulls at my attention, so I turn my thoughts towards it then something stops me.

It's like an alarm, a warning?

"I feel something Silas," I say.

"That would be expected, I think," he chuckles.

"Not that," I say, sitting up and slapping his chest lightly. "Something is—"

I'm cut off by a scraping, screeching sound. Metal being torn apart. Something is here. We've been found.

I leap to my feet and grab clothes. Silas is right behind me, though his pants go on smoother than mine. I'm hopping foot to foot as I try to pull the damn things on, but they've turned inside out and it's mission impossible.

The sounds of screeching and metal tearing heighten. Magic crawls along my skin, the buzz of it rattles my bones, ready to be unleashed. I'm going to tear apart whatever is attacking us. I don't care if I have to do it half-naked. Whatever it is, it's going to pay!

There's a knock on the door as my pants finally obey, sliding up into place.

"Come in!" I yell jerking the shirt over my head.

Silas, amazingly, is already dressed. Does he have a spell? Shit.

Rafe throws the door open, his dark, fiery eyes taking in my state of dress in an instant. A lascivious grin forms on his face.

"No time, you naughty kids," he teases. "Bigger fish to fry."

"What is it?" I ask, pushing past him into the hall.

"Mutant birds, of all things," he says as I turn left at a run.

He grabs my shoulder, spins me around. Magic flares as my focus is shifted to his hand.

"Not that way," he says.

"That's where the sounds are!" I yell.

He moves so quick it's a blur, stepping around me and blocking my path forward.

"There are more that way," he says pointing behind us.

"What are you hiding?" I ask, suspicious, pushing into him and trying to get past.

"No time to argue details, girl," he says, pointing back the other way again. "Seriously, we need you up front, that way we've got covered."

I'm suspicious, and look at him through narrowed eyes, but if nothing else he's right, now isn't the time for arguing. Spinning on my heel, I bolt towards the front of the train.

CHAPTER TWELVE

NATHANIAL

*T*he tearing sounds were the first alarm. We should have known sooner. Something or someone must have disabled some of the wards. We're already in a precarious situation without someone onboard actively working against us. I step between two cars, unfold my wings, and take to the air to assess the threat.

Mutant trumpet-creatures that might once have been birds tear at the train cars. Sharp talons rip the steel, leaving long scars in the smooth metal. They dive in and out, a swirling flock, and with each pass they cut deeper through the roof. They'll be inside shortly.

A group of them breaks off from the flock, flying for me. I draw my magic together so my wings glow bright white, and I summon my sword to fend them off with. The flaming blade appears in my hand, as I take on a ready stance.

They're not intelligent. Something sent them or else it's bad luck, but they have an animal cunning. They separate, swirling through the air around me. Five of them dive and climb in an impressive aerial acrobatics display intended to distract me and create an opening for one of them.

They screech and caw to each other in a crude form of language unique to them. I don't give them time to play their game. Aviella is in danger. I fly higher, pulling them up and away from the train and giving myself room to maneuver.

Once high enough, I engage. Thrusting my fiery blade at the closest but not committing to the motion as I turn it the instant the one behind me dives in to attack. The blade swings around and I lop off its taloned feet.

It screeches in surprise, then pain, and drops from the sky, unable to control itself any longer. Four to go. Beneath me on the train, I see Rafe and Aviella emerge with Silas. More of the birds move to attack them. Behind the birds, mostly blocked from view, a handful of dead people and undead monstrosities crawl along the roof, making their way for the ripped openings.

Intelligent. Too intelligent.

This is no accident or bad luck. This is planned.

My blood runs cold but there isn't time as another of the creatures dives in, immediately followed by the rest. They're not taking chances, all of them closing at once despite the risk of interfering with each other's ability to fly.

I close my eyes and shift all my senses to my magic. Let them come. When they are close enough, I open my eyes and let loose the golden light of the Divine flame that powers me. It explodes out in a ring around me and they burst into puffs of dust as it consumes them.

I'm high above the train looking down on the battle below. Rafe is fighting three of them. I wince as one takes a bite out of his arm, and he cries out in pain.

Aviella battles to his side, wielding magic around her as if it's the most natural thing to her in the world. She is a goddess marching across a field of battle. Glowing in my eyes, her magic a beacon, and I'm not the only one who sees it.

The flock is drawn to her. As a group they swirl up into the air. A black blight against the sky forming an arrow aiming for Aviella.

My heart leaps into my throat as the flock dances and swerves. Leaning forward, adrenaline pumping, I fold my wings and dive. I know there is no way I will reach her in time, but I have to try. Aviella spins around, finishing the one in front of her. Even from here I see her eyes widen when she sees the flock coming. Then she smiles.

Her arms weave through the air, pulling power as she draws symbols that I've taught her.

The flock crashes into her barrier, repelling most of them. Only four make it past. Air rushes past, thrumming in my ears in time with the racing of my heart. With my own magic I will myself to be faster, but some laws are not as mutable as others and I gain no speed.

Rafe leaps to her aid, tackling one of the monstrous birds and driving it away from her. Three face her as I close. Her magic flares bright, golden-white, almost blinding. One of the three falls back screeching. Two left, and I'm too far. Too far to help. Closing my eyes for an instant, I offer a plea for help to the Divine.

No response returns to my plea. I'm left to do all I can as fate unfolds before me. Is this it? Will she fall? Her hands glow—then she smiles.

"Come get it," she growls, dashing forward.

Her glowing fist drives through the skull of one opponent. The other tears at her with its talons, ripping through cloth and flesh. Blood sprays as she cries out her pain.

Whirling, she slams her fist into the monster's chest. Yelling a battle cry, she rips its heart out. The creature drops to the top of the racing train car, lifeless.

Aviella stumbles back, holding the heart in her hands. Blood splatters across her clothes and face, her energy wavers. Landing behind her I wrap her in my arms, steadying her.

"Thanks," she says, wiping an arm across her forehead.

"That was fun," Rafe says sarcastically.

"We need to get back inside," I say, swaying with the rocking of the train.

"Are they gone?" Aviella asks, looking around.

The rushing wind blows her hair around forming it into a halo, and she looks, for all the world, like an angel. As if she could be my own kin. Something formed of the Divine itself, not of mortal flesh or at least not completely. She's a stern, haughty, goddess of war, no longer the scared young girl I first met.

Admiration fills my heart, and my body reacts with desire to express my love with her mortal coil. Now, of all times, I'm finding it harder and harder to control my impulses, but I know now is not the time. Not yet. Fate has plans for her that will only be revealed to me when my part is clear. Until then her path is clouded to me.

"For now," Rafe says, an ominous edge to his voice. He pushes one of the bodies with the toe of his boot. "I'm sure we'll have more fun before the ride is over."

"Great," Aviella says grimly. She turns a slow circle as she pushes away from me. "It still feels like…."

"Like what?" I ask.

"Watched," she says, frowning. "Like we're being watched."

An eerie shiver passes down my spine as I nod my understanding. I can't disagree with her assessment. Something does seem to be watching us, but who or what?

The three of us climb down and go into the train car. Efram and Silas are entering from the other side, also covered in the grime of battle.

"Are you okay?" Efram asks as he pushes past Silas and runs to Aviella.

"I'm fine," she says, shaking her head.

"Let me have that," Silas says, pointing to her hand that still holds the heart.

She looks at her hand as if she's forgotten it was hers or that she's holding a heart in it. Shrugging, she hands it to Silas who produces a linen bag from somewhere and motions for her to drop it in. Sealing the bag, which has the soft glow of his magic on it, he hands the bag to Efram.

"Read that," he orders.

Efram nods agreement, takes it, but never removes his attention from Aviella.

"What about the others?" she asks.

"You should shower," I say, placing a hand on her arm. She doesn't want to know. Doesn't need to know. I felt the souls leaving. This has been a massacre. She jerks away. "No. Tell me."

Her voice is firm, an order, not a question. The four of us look at each other, then Efram speaks.

"I don't know yet," he admits.

She nods, grim. "Fine. Find out, I want a count of how many we lost by the time I'm done showering."

Efram and Silas both look surprised, but Rafe is grinning. She's becoming a leader.

"Right," Efram says, turning to leave.

"Somehow, this has to stop," she says, the barest hint of despair in her voice as she turns and walks to the shower.

CHAPTER THIRTEEN

SILAS

There is too much symbology.

We've gathered the fallen with the help of the surviving passengers into a single car. The train slows as we grimly wait next to the pile of dead. We can't keep them on the train for multiple reasons. I would throw them off without ceremony—dead bodies are no longer the person—but Aviella would not hear of it.

She's sleeping now, and we all decided it was the best time to handle this, while she wouldn't have to be directly involved. Knowing the scope of loss is much different than having to face it head on. There are bodies of all ages in this pile. The Shadow Forces do not discriminate in any manner.

The number of survivors is symbolic. Twenty-one. A holy number, divisible by three. The Trinity. Once the last person had fallen, the dead things pulled back and there is no doubt in my mind it was not because of Efram's and my defense. The goal of the Shadow had been accomplished.

Turning the number over and over in my head I try to grasp the significance. As it doesn't come clear I look earlier. Often times the answer starts earlier than you suspect. A key concept for one truly trying to understand life and the universe.

A single murder. One done on the train by one of our own survivors. I know, thanks to Rafe, that it was manipulated by the Shadow Forces. Why?

There's only one clear answer that makes sense. Aviella is at the center of everything. So the murder must have been to push her. Push her to what?

Scar her. Steel her. Prepare her….

The train jerks to a stop with a last squeal of the wheels. Efram slides the side cargo door open as Nathanial orders the survivors into lines. We pass the fallen down the line to form a pile. We don't have time for a mass grave, but we can give them what respect possible. We'll burn the bodies and say the rites that will help them to pass over.

The last thing we need to do is fuel the Shadow powers with more bodies. It's hard, sweaty work, but we finish it as fast as possible. Several of the survivors have tears streaming down their faces as they work. One breaks down completely when handling a particular body.

It catches at my attention, the way they're reacting. I've grown cold to the loss of bodies. Too many years, too many losses, they do not affect me so strongly.

Aviella isn't cold, though. She's closer to these survivors than I am by far. Closer than any of us. An angel, a demon, a necroseer even are all so used to death that its action doesn't faze us. That's the point. They're making her colder.

"Right!" I exclaim as the idea becomes clear.

"Right?" Efram asks.

"I see it now," I say. "The goal, the purpose of these attacks."

We continue passing the bodies down the line, but the other men watch me waiting for my explanation.

"Care to explain that there, Silas?" Rafe asks.

"Of course," I say. "We know the goal is Aviella, but why? What does this accomplish?"

I point at the bodies around us.

"Weakening out potential allies?" Efram asks and Rafe snorts.

"These aren't allies," I say shaking my head. "Look at them, no magic, no powers to aid us. They're survivors, and barely that. None of them would survive on their own. No, that isn't it at all."

Efram flushes with anger or embarrassment, but doesn't say more.

"So what then?" Nathanial asks.

"To make her cold," I explain.

"Cold?" Rafe asks.

"Yes, exactly. Where does Aviella draw—"

"Where do I draw what?" she asks, surprising me by showing up behind me.

Everyone stops to look. "I thought you were asleep," I say.

"I was," she says. "But the train stopped."

Her eyes wander over the remaining bodies, only a few, we were almost done. If we'd been faster, we could have protected her from this. My chest aches, but there's nothing I can do.

"You should go back to your room," Nathanial says.

Her eyes lock onto him, bright and glittering with unshed tears.

"No," she shakes her head. "I should be part of this."

CHAPTER FOURTEEN

EFRAM

*M*y heart shatters seeing the look on her face. It hurts so bad tears well in my eyes too. The pain she feels is palpable, echoing into her magic, swirling around each of us. My throat closes and I can't speak so I do the only thing I can.

I walk to her, arms open, wanting to embrace her. To, somehow, take the load of this pain from her. As I come closer though, the shine of what I thought was tears in her eyes—isn't. Her eyes harden as I watch, and her face becomes colder.

"We can't dig a grave," she remarks, her voice cold. "It will take too long."

"We know," Nathanial says.

"Fire?" she asks, casually.

The survivors watch the interplay between those of us on the train. They're tired, exhausted is more accurate, and emotionally drained. These are the friends, family, even lovers that we're discussing so casually. They don't have tears left to shed though.

"Yes," Silas says.

The despair from the survivors is a fog overlaying everything. Magically it feels as thick as a pea-soup, making everything harder.

"Let's finish this," she says.

She doesn't move into my open arms, so I let them drop, feeling foolish. When she looks up at me her eyes are dull, lifeless. Almost dead, as if she's donned an emotional armor that has driven her deep and away from her humanity.

Oh.

That's what Silas was meaning. Glancing at the Methuselah, I arch an eyebrow. He seems to understand my inherent question as he grimaces and nods.

The Shadow is pushing her away from her humanity. How long can anyone face despair and still cling to hope? How many losses before you give up on faith? How many people can you fail to save before you become too cold and hard to be a hero any longer?

It's clear as day, now that I see it. The manipulations, the death, the constant push and keeping us only one step ahead. Every time we've found a safe haven having only enough time to get somewhat comfortable, to form connections, then have them ripped away.

Oh Aviella.

"You're getting stronger," I tell her.

She glances over and nods, then grabs the legs of a body. I help her to carry it to the line, where it's placed on the pile. We finish the last few, then climb off the train and stand before the gruesome pile. Silence lies heavy, broken only by the soft sounds of crying from the survivors.

Aviella takes a step forward and turns to face the group. Behind her rises the pile of bodies accenting her grim face.

"I'm sorry," she says, shaking her head but meeting the gaze of each person gathered. "I'm sorry I've failed you."

No one speaks, stunned into silence by her words.

"Aviella," Rafe says. "This isn't your fault."

"Isn't it?" she counters. "Isn't it all my fault?"

Her hands ball into fists and take on the soft glow of her magic. The swell of it washes over me, refreshing and terrifying in its strength at the same time. She's pulling more power than I've ever felt her wield before.

"What are we supposed to do now?" someone from the twenty-one survivors asks.

Aviella grimaces, facing them all, then she does something unexpected. Their despair, she pulls it from them. It passes over me, making my knees weak to the point it's all I can do to remain standing. She drags it out and as she does it dissipates, but her magic grows stronger. It's as if she's feeding on their despair, turning it to power. I glance at Silas who's watching her interestedly.

"We prepare," Aviella growls.

Her aura grows brighter until it's almost blinding, I lower my magical sight, unable to gaze on her any longer with it. The bodies behind her smolder then in a whoosh catch on fire, blazing in an instant. The flames reach for the sky like orange arms clawing their way into the heavens. The fiery glow outlines Aviella and for an instant she is a dark goddess walking out of hell, surrounded by the flames of eternal fire.

"We fight," she yells, raising one glowing fist to the sky.

The survivors cheer as the flames behind her shoot up in response to her gesture as if in their own agreement. She strides past me, and a cold chill passes over my skin as she does.

Silas may be right. Her humanity, her love for everyone, is what makes her special. Can she lose that? Can we save her from it?

Doubts assail my thoughts as I watch her stride through the small crowd and back onto the train. She doesn't look back once.

Oh God, please protect her. Aviella I'm here for you. I only hope it's enough.

CHAPTER FIFTEEN

AVIELLA

The whispers won't stop. I'm not sure if they're the dead whispering to me or my own delusions. The despair of the survivors tasted sweet, like cool water when you're thirsty. It doesn't last though. Isn't strong enough to outdo the empty aching loss in my own guts.

It's enough. I've got to get over death. It's all around us, waiting at every turn. It's time to accept that I can't save them all, no matter how hard I try. Every time I let my guard down, even for an instant, the Shadow is there, ready to pounce. Stealing away everything I care for, everything that matters.

Every precaution taken, doing our best to be so careful, but none of it matters. None of it stops them from taking from me, without consideration. I can't even slow them down!

I slam my fist into the wall. Stars explode in my head as the pain radiates up my arm. It's a good pain. A centering pain. Pain is what I deserve. Anger burns as I stare at my blood-covered hand. I'm dancing on the edge of a darkness that I don't know how to control. At times I don't feel like myself.

The whispers continue. Failure. Loser. It's over. Give up. Save me. Where were you? Droning on and on like a mosquito buzzing in my ear, but it's in my head and I can't make it stop. I don't know what to do, what's next, or how to save them.

They don't deserve this, no one does. Being dragged through the depths of some kind of hell, all because I wasn't ready. Again. My magic is a swirling storm waiting to break. I pull it up and surround myself in it like armor made of lightning. The constant noise telling me I failed fades to background noise. I shake my head, clear my throat, square my shoulders, and pull my shit together. I can't afford to wallow in self-pity.

Twenty-one. The number is a cold, hard reality. Twenty-one survivors are all that's left. Maybe they'll find comfort in the Mega-church. New Jerusalem will be a shock for them, but if they're real survivors, they'll adapt. Maybe some faith is what we all need?

Faith.

Do I have any? What do I believe? I'm lost, abandoned, but I'm not alone. None of that answers the question though, does it. Do I believe?

It should be easy, really. I travel with a demon and an angel. How can I not believe in God? Well it's not that I don't believe in God, really. It's more... is this all part of his plan? Why? Why would any caring, loving God do this to his people? This doesn't even feel like a vengeful god, no, this feels like something that...

What?

Frowning I try to pull the feeling into words, something that I can understand. It's almost too big, elusive, slipping through my thoughts but too hard to form it. It feels like something that wants to eat the world. Destroy it for no other reason than it exists.

That doesn't sound like a God, certainly not a benevolent one. There's more to this than I can comprehend yet. Some machination or motivation that doesn't add up. Silas had me read, a lot, and one thing I did figure out is that most of the Bible as I knew it drew off of even older stories.

Maybe our ideas of spirituality are too diluted. Obviously, Nate knows more than he's telling me, but Rafe is always open about things. Could he shed more light for me? Or would he deflect and distract, which is more usual for him.

All the stories have parallels or origins far back. Even the resurrection traces back to Inanna, where she died and rose three days later. Cain and Abel are reminiscent of Osiris and Set. Either one story is derived from the prior or...

Or we keep repeating the same cycles over and over. Creation, stories, attempts to save the creation, failures to save the creation, destruction.

Do we really keep repeating the same mistakes? That's taking the old maxim of those who don't study history are doomed to repeat it to an extreme. My own story, this mystical 'fate' pulling me along doesn't seem to have a direct parallel. Maybe I'm wrong, but Dad taught me a lot of biblical stories and while a lot of the Apocalypse lines up with the Revelation, I don't seem to have fit into it.

So where does that leave me? Lost. Check. Delusional? Maybe. Maybe that's all it is. What if I'm actually in a looney-bin, straitjacket and all, this is some mental construct in my own mind to protect myself from whatever drove me crazy.

Except my hand throbs with pain where I slammed the wall. No. This is real. Too real, but real all the same. Outside my magic barrier, the whispers keep a steady level of white noise but beyond them is the grief, loss, and despair of the survivors.

They've lost friends, family, lovers, and they're about to give up. Their emotions wash through the train like a torrential rain pouring down in sheets. Each pass over swamps in, pushing against me, assaulting as it intertwines and mixes with my own feelings. It's impossible to feel... free. I'm not certain, that's what bothers me the most. I'm not sure what's next. Where do we go? Is the Mega-church where my Dad is? Is it the right move, or am I bringing danger to another bunker? Will it fall like those that came before it?

Closing my eyes, I take in a deep breath then slowly let it out. I take another and do the same, willing my heart to quit racing. When I open my eyes, I'm calmer. I should clean up. I'm a mess from the battle, which can't be helping my overall mood.

"I'll do my best," I say it out loud, defiant. "I'll protect them to the best of my ability."

Decision made, I leave my small room and head for the bathroom, so I can shower. I'm almost to the room when something changes in the whispers. I can't make it out inside the protective shell of magic I've armored myself into. Curiosity gets the best of me and I let my armor soften.

Aviella....

Dad?

Aviella.... Careful....

"Daddy!" I cry out, tears welling in my eyes.

As fast as I say his name, though, the whisper is gone, replaced by the accusations of the dead. Or the Shadow Forces. Whatever it is, my heart pounds as I strain to hear his voice, willing him to talk to me. Willing him to be alive and be okay.

That empty ache and sense of loss forms familiarly into my guts, and I push ahead into the bathroom. The wavy mirror distorts my reflection making me look, I hope, worse than I do. I fill the sink with water, then splash it on my face.

As the water falls back into the basin, it quickly turns pink. I wash up the best I can, then stare at myself in the mirror.

I look better. Mostly.

It's been hard, such a hard journey, so much loss. I can't let it get to me though. The Shadow wants me to despair. That I'm certain about. Everything else may be up in the air, but there is no doubt I'm a target, and that the best way for them to win is for me to give up.

The hairs on the back of my neck stand on end as if I'm being watched. There's a sensation of that which makes my skin crawl. Am I? A light brush as if someone caresses my skin, but no, it's not my skin. It's my thoughts. As if someone is trying to read my thoughts!

Gasping, heart pounding, I turn in a fast circle. Who?

There's no one here with me in the small room. I'm alone. The sensation recedes as if aware of my having found it out. I don't know what that was, but it's creepy and I don't like it. Stay the hell out of my head!

Distracted, I slam the door open, storm out, and bounce off of Rafe.

"Well, hello," he says, grinning. "Fancy meeting you here."

"Rafe," I bark, catching myself from falling back into the bathroom on my ass. "Damn it, you startled me."

"I'm sorry," he says, without a hint of remorse in his voice.

"Why are you here?" I ask.

"Why are any of us here?" he asks, tilting his head to one side as he waxes philosophic. "That's really the question, isn't it?"

His eyes smolder, and before I can retort with some smart-ass remark, he moves closer. The air is sucked out of my lungs by his presence. Magic soothes across my skin, embracing me. He steps right into my personal space, so close I can't take my eyes off the fire burning in his black eyes.

"Pleasure," he says, his voice husky and low. "Pleasure is why we're here, if you're wondering."

His burning fingers touch my cheek and I flush, heart racing, breath catching. Instant desire rushes through me. Nothing could be better than taking Rafe, giving myself over to the pleasing sensations I know he is capable of. He's a kind and attentive lover, and what better way to push back the despair and overwhelm than taking control of my own body and using his?

He bends into me, his lips brushing mine as his hot breath passes over my skin. He places feather light touches up and down my arms, his lips just touching mine, my cheek, the tip of my nose.

My body melds against his as he wraps an arm around my waist pulling me in. I'm burning with aching need. The whispers of the lost are gone, driven away by his magic joining with mine. The dark despair, he takes it from me, unburdening my load.

"Rafe," I whisper.

"Aviella," he whispers my name in return, but it carries so much more than a single word should.

It's an oath, a confession, a demand even. He wants me, needs me, and he's not going to be denied. He moves, suddenly, grabbing my arms where they hang at my sides and forcing them over my head. He presses against me, forcing me back into the bathroom.

We crash against the wall, his body pinning me in place. He grasps my wrists with one hand and his free hand moves over my body, between us, until it's between my legs rubbing hard against my hidden mound.

"Mmm-uhhh," I groan, eyes rolling up in my head.

He kisses my neck, rough. He's unshaven, the bristles sandpaper against my skin, only making it all hotter. He thrusts his hips in, driving his hard cock into my stomach while his hand continues to rub furiously.

I can't get a deep breath, panting, I need him. Now. In me.

Our magic is two mighty forces, slamming one into another over and over. Crashing like waves against the beach. Coming together, but not penetrating, like our bodies. I need him to penetrate me. I need to claim him, again.

I try to break my hands free, but he tightens his grip, growling. His burning eyes lock onto mine, and he shakes his head.

"No," he hisses. "You're mine."

Anger flashes, but it's instantly replaced by a sensation of dominance. He's in control, and suddenly I retreat and give it to him.

Biting my lip I nod, and then give myself over to the pleasures he's going to bring. He stops rubbing between my legs, his hand moving up to my pants and undoing them.

He slides them partway down, far enough he can slide his finger under them and then drive it into my wet, waiting pussy.

"Ah!" I cry out as a wave of relief rushes through, bucking my hips to drive his fingers in deeper.

"Yes," he growls.

He rubs up and down, pushing his fingers in deep then dragging them sweetly back out and across my clit, until I'm dancing on the edge of exploding. Right there and then he stops without warning, pulling his hand free.

I gasp, so close to my pleasure, it leaves me aching.

"Rafe, please," I beg.

He grins and shakes his head. "Not yet."

His mouth closes with mine, claiming my lips. his tongue drives past my lips and finds mine pushing ahead to meet him. We kiss with a passion that edges towards something uncontrollable. Wild, rough, our magic twines, twisting around but still not penetrating.

He takes a step back, coming up against the sink in the small space. His eyes burn as he looks me up and down in my half-dressed state.

"Beautiful," he says, his voice throaty. I flush with pleasure and embarrassment both. "You are perfect. Show me more, take it off... slowly."

I hesitate. I've never been an exhibitionist but focusing on him grounds me in the now. And I like the way he looks at me, the way his eyes dance with delight and desire. The look on his face is one of worship. Trailing my hands down my sides I pinch the hem of my shirt and lift it slowly up, wriggling my hips as my breasts come free.

The shirt tangles my arms over my head, and it takes a moment for me to get them free. Rafe's eyes burn, his lips are parted, and then one-handed he undoes his pants, and his impressive cock drops free. He doesn't take his eyes off of me as he takes it in his hand and unhurriedly strokes.

"More," he says, his voice deep.

Seeing him pleasure himself looking at me awakens a sense of power in me. I reach out to him with my magic and lightly stroke his cock, as I hook my already open pants with my thumbs.

Gradually, teasingly, I push them down. He strokes faster as I rotate my hips.

My pants fall to my ankles and I step out of them. Leaning my shoulders against the wall I angle my hips out and spread my legs. Running my fingers over my pussy, lightly touching the clit, with each stroke I bite my lip to hold back a cry of pleasure.

It's almost too much instantly. His magic flows over my skin, the softest of touches that accents every sensation, as if his body was pressing against me softly.

I push two fingers into my hot pussy, amazed at how wet and warm I am. He groans, stroking faster, watching me. His magic rises and mine races to keep up with it. I embrace him across the small space and as my magic connects with his, the sensations of his body become mine.

The pleasure is doubling over, it's too much. I'm fighting to not go over the edge. It's too hard. There's no way to keep myself.

"Uhn," he grunts, feeling it too.

He rushes across the room, hooking my ass and lifting me up. He shoves his cock into me deep and hard.

That's it. Pleasure explodes as we fall over the edge together into our shared orgasm. The magic makes his orgasm mine and mine his. All thought is gone, exploded away in the shock waves. I'm left shuddering, a shivering wreck and if he wasn't holding me up, I'm sure I'd be on the floor A quivering pile of pleasured flesh.

Finally I pull myself up by grabbing him by his neck. We unentangle ourselves, and I lean against him waiting for the weakness in my knees to pass. Once I've caught my breath, I chuckle.

"That was different," I say, resting my head on his chest and listening to his pounding heart.

"Are you okay?" he asks.

"Yes," I say. "I think so anyway."

"Good," he says, holding me silently. "You have to be careful."

"That's broad," I say.

"Yeah," he breathes into my hair, his fingers running through it. "Don't feed into the illusions. That's how they work. Whispers, urges, subtle directions that you react to, and it seems so reasonable, like it's the right action."

"Rafe, what are you talking about?" I ask, raising my head off his chest.

His eyes search mine, looking for something. He smiles, his easygoing, infectious grin.

"Nothing," he says enigmatically. "Or maybe everything. It's how they work, that's all."

"They?" I ask.

"The Shadow, as you call them," he says. "You know… my people."

"I never lump you in with the Shadow," I say trailing a hand down his cheek.

He smiles, takes my hand in his and kisses my palm while shaking his head.

"Ah, dear Aviella," he says. "I am though, no matter if you lump me in with them or not. I am what I am. A demon. A fearsome creature from the depths."

"You're better than that," I say, pulling my hand out of his and grabbing him by his chin, forcing him to look directly at me.

"Am I?" he asks, his voice so soft I barely hear it.

"Yes," I say with total certainty.

"One of us will betray you, Avi," he says. "It will happen, willful or not, intended or not. Our opposition is… powerful. More powerful than I think you realize."

"I don't care," I say, eyes narrowing, "how powerful it is. We can't fail. The fate of the world is at stake."

"It is," he agrees. "So heed my words. Do not feed into the illusions, the whispers. A campaign of doubt is a key of their arsenal. Believe in yourself, let the rest of us be damned."

We stare until his eyes soften, and then he leans in and kisses me. It's not as filled with hot passion as his kisses normally are. This is something different. It's loving, soft, tender in a way that is unusual for Rafe.

"You bring out the best in us," he says. "The best in me. You make me a better man."

"We're going to win," I say.

"Perhaps," he shrugs, stepping away from me and pulling up his pants. "Win or lose, we'll do it together."

"Win or lose," I agree, feeling cold, calm, and yet terrified at the same time.

I watch the demon out of the corner of my eye while I pull on my clothes. He's distracted, and there's an air of uncertainty that I've never felt from him before. When he catches me looking his face lights up in a smile and the sensation is gone.

"We got this," he says, putting an arm around my shoulder.

"We do," I agree, but the doubts in the back of my mind are loud, not whispers but the screams of the damned demanding attention.

The only way is forward. Save my Dad, then we'll see what's next.

CHAPTER SIXTEEN

AVIELLA

*M*y stolen moment with Rafe was both satisfying and not at the same time. It left me feeling contemplative and introspective. I keep replaying his words over and over. One thing stood out only after he'd left to do… whatever it is he does when he's not with me.

One of us will betray you.

How can he know that? Which one? What can I do about it?

The mood of the train is somber. Twenty-one survivors put out fewer emotions than the over-packed train of before, but what they are feeling is strong. It's like the current of a strong river running around my legs, tugging me along, wanting me to go in the same direction with it.

I've found a window seat to myself where I watch the landscape rolling by while drinking coffee. Coffee reminds me of my Dad. He loved coffee so much. We had so many breakfasts at roadside diners that it seems most of my memories of him are in one or another. He'd always have coffee and after the waitress left, he'd raise the cup, take a deep sniff, then smile and take his first sip.

"That's the nectar," he'd say.

A smile plays across my lips, tugging at the corners as I relive the memory of him. His voice was deep, rich, resonating through me. Dad. Protector, but now he needs me. All the years on the road with him seemed normal, natural, because what other life did I know?

He was preparing me. Getting me ready for this. I shake my head and sigh. There's a sick odor that's like a thick layer of smog. We're deep into Wormwood territory now, and besides the bird attack it's been uneventful. So far.

Looking out the window is depressing. The land is black and flat. The only thing breaking up the black is green, slimy-looking pools that glow. Radiation, for sure. Here, where the government was experimenting with all kinds of sick things. Surprise! Look what happens when a secret project gets out of control.

In most ways, the entire Apocalypse started right here in this area. Maybe it was fate though. I can't argue whether it was a self-fulfilling prophecy. Some bastard naming the secret research center Wormwood probably thought he was being clever. Well done, unknown person, you found a beautiful symmetry that contributed to the end of the world.

"Hey, I've made soup," Efram says, walking into the car I'd had to myself.

He holds out a steaming bowl which I take gratefully. He sits down across from me, holding a bowl for himself. I smile and thank him but can't think of anything more to say. I take a spoonful and blow to cool it off, letting my thoughts wander as I enjoy the comfort of his presence, but more the silence. It's like being alone without the downsides.

"Supplies are low, we'll probably be doing soup the rest of the way," he comments, setting aside his empty bowl.

"I thought we had plenty?" I ask.

He frowns. "We did."

"What happened?" I ask.

"It's hard to tell, but a lot of what we had spoiled," he says. "We've got enough, but it's best to be cautious."

"Okay," I say, trusting him and the boys to handle the logistics.

At least they're not hiding it from me. That's good.

"Are you... okay?" he asks, switching seats to sit next to me.

I pull my legs up under myself to make room for him. I pause to think about it. Am I okay? Everyone asks me that a lot. Maybe I am, maybe I'm broken.

"Yeah," I say at last.

"Good," he says, not pressing. "It's going to get rough, you know."

"Yeah," I agree. "We'll get through it."

He smiles and my heart melts. Efram and I haven't joined yet but the connection between us is stronger than probably any of the others. He's been with me since this crazy journey started. He was the first.

"Efram," I say, soft, unsure what I'm going to say next.

"Yes," he smiles.

"Are you okay?" I ask.

His eyes cloud over as he thinks about it. His body quivers and drifts closer.

"I am," he says at last. "As well as can be."

"Right," I say, looking out the window. "You see all that?"

I'm changing the subject and we both know it, but he goes along with it.

"What about it?" he asks.

"I was thinking about the symmetry of it, the idea of a self-fulfilling prophecy, you know?"

"In what way?" he asks.

"The government code-named this Project Wormwood. Wormwood, like in the Bible, the star that crashes to earth."

"Right?" he asks.

"What do you think this looked like when it exploded? When their experiments broke free?"

He stares at the window and shakes his head.

"What about it, Aviella?" he asks.

"In my reading and training with Silas, I've learned, at its core, magic is all intention. What do you intend to happen?"

"I can see that," Efram nods.

"Like your magic, while it's limited to a specific area, you have talents that work with that particular type of energy, and your intention is what makes the effect."

"Okay," he says. "I follow."

"What did they intend here? How do we know they didn't intend an end-of-the-world scenario? Knowingly or unknowingly."

He looks out the window at the rolling terrain. He doesn't speak for a long time, and I let him stew the idea over.

"There was a mindset of... last strike," he says.

"Last strike?" I ask, unfamiliar with the term.

"The idea that if we ever got into a nuclear war, that the world would be over," he says. "I always thought that's what the Apocalypse would be or would be triggered by anyway. The idea that if the enemy launched missiles at the United States there would be a retaliatory strike-back fully intended to end the offending country."

"Wow," I say. "That's insane."

"It was, or it is," he agrees. "The depths of insanity and destruction mankind is capable of is surprising at times."

"Well that's my point," I say. "There was some kind of intention behind the name. The idea this is it, the doomsday scenario if you will."

"Yeah," he says. "Deep thoughts, Aviella."

"Yeah," I agree, shifting in the seat so I can lean against him.

He wraps an arm around my shoulder, and we stare out the window together. We ride along in comfortable silence, but one thing keeps digging at me.

"Efram?" I ask.

"Hmm?"

"Is there anything else you guys are hiding from me?" I ask.

He's silent but I feel his heart rate increase. I don't need my magic to know he's debating lying to me or to tell when he settles on the truth.

"There was a murder," he says. "Before the attack."

"A murder?" I ask.

"Yeah," he agrees.

"Who did it?" I ask.

"She's among the peaceful now," he says.

Part of me feels like I should probe deeper, but if they've handled it, why? What good does it do me to know more?

"Okay," I say, sighing heavily.

It's another blow, but my life has been nothing but one blow after another. I'm afraid I'm getting numb to the loss. That's probably my biggest fear right now. Sooner or later, I'll be so numb none of it will matter.

"How do you do it?" I ask at last.

"Do what?" he asks.

"Deal with death all the time and not grow cold from it?"

"Death is part of life," he says, hugging me tighter. "The ones I deal with cry out for justice. I don't care what the poets say, justice isn't cold. It's life, it's balancing the scales. If you're trying to balance scales, to make life have purpose and meaning and make even death be meaningful, how can you grow cold?"

"Huh," I say, thinking over his answer, but then a yawn takes me by surprise.

"You should sleep," he says.

"Yeah," I agree, snuggling up to him more.

He kisses my forehead, and I drift to sleep safe in his arms.

CHAPTER SEVENTEEN

SILAS

Keeping shadows pulled around me, I watch Aviella and Efram. She needs him. He provides her a comfort that is natural and easy. Rafe can take her pain away, but it's an anodyne that is magic based. What Efram gives her comes purely from his heart and the connection the two of them share.

A sharp stab of jealousy hits me in the chest. I wish I could be that for her. Be the rock she depends on, the one she can lean into, but that is not who I am. No, that is Efram's role in our harem, and I am smart enough to not begrudge him his place.

It's important we each know our role. We don't have time for petty in-squabbling. The forces arrayed against us are too much for that. I've survived by maintaining strict control. Control of everything, but most especially my feelings.

I let myself open up to her and look what happened. We were attacked, and I was caught unaware. It won't happen again.

She snuggles up, resting her head on his chest. My arms

ache to hold her, but I won't wallow in self-pity. Protecting her is more important. I slip through the car and leave, letting them have their moment together. She needs the sleep as it is.

The shadow cloak lets me move through the passengers unnoticed. I scan their emotional states with my magic, gauging how they're feeling and what they're likely to do. Despair is first and foremost. They seem to have given up even on their game of being 'best' among each other.

The sadness they feel is overwhelming, but a three of them are more than sad. They're angry, boiling, and leaning into the dark whispers.

The one thing I couldn't explain to the others about Wormwood is the effect I feared it might have on the passengers. It wasn't something I could put into words, more feelings and instinct. Now that I see it in action, I've got a better handle on it.

So much evil happened in this area that the very air is tainted with it. The experiments that were being done before the Apocalypse were illegal, unethical, and, calling a spade a spade, evil. Torture was the lowest of the crimes being done here daily.

It's left its mark, and I have no doubts that this was if not the, one of the gates that let the Shadow into this realm.

Three of the passengers are ready to explode. I don't want to act prematurely. I'm still puzzling out the exactness of twenty-one of them being left alive. I don't know if that was by design of Shadow or Light. I do not believe it was coincidence. I've lived too long for that.

I seek out Rafe by extending my senses until I recognize his signature further ahead. I follow my instinct until I'm standing between cars, looking into the one ahead and not seeing him. Closing my eyes helps me narrow in his location.

Up.

Odd. I climb the ladder next to the door. When I stick my head over the top of the car, wind blows hard against me, mussing my hair. Irritating.

Rafe is standing on the roof at the front of the car. He has his arms spread, his head thrown back, and I'm not sure he's not screaming into the wind with the words being carried away by it or not. The rattle of the train cars down the track are loud out here and combined with the rush of air I'd never hear it anyway.

Carefully I climb up onto the roof and using magic to stick my feet I walk to the demon. He turns before I reach him, dark eyes smoldering, with a wide grin on his face. His demonic presence is stronger than he usually lets out.

"Rafe," I yell to be heard.

"Can you feel it?" he asks, arms still wide.

"Yes," I agree.

"Of course you can, Methuselah. It calls to me. The darkness here, do you know that? It's a sirens call, pulling me towards it."

"You're not the only one," I say grimly.

"No? Passengers about to crack, are they?" he asks.

"Three of them," I say. "I need you to keep an eye on them."

"I could handle it," he says.

"No," I order.

His grin widens. "You would stop me?"

"No," I say. "I wouldn't, but she will."

The grin falters and the burning fire in his eyes dims as he regains control over his baser instincts.

"She would, wouldn't she?" he asks. "How does she do it, Silas? Despite everything, every betrayal, every terrible human foible, she still loves them."

"That is what makes her special," I say.

He nods, frowning deep in thought. "It is."

"Can you watch them?" I ask.

"Of course," he says. "I've got an eye on them already."

"Good," I tell him and turn to go back inside.

It's what I can do for now. I can't let my guard down again. For her sake.

CHAPTER EIGHTEEN

NATHANIAL

The demon's magic repels against mine. Opposites repelling each other like two opposed magnets. The sense of him is always clear. I know exactly where he is. Now he's one car ahead of me, casually patrolling through the handful of survivors.

He gave me Silas's warning, not that I needed it. These survivors are an oddity. In part, they feel as if they're touched by fate, a hint of the Divine but they're still filled with darkness. It's not that I haven't sensed this before. Some paths the Divine takes are... difficult to comprehend, but then comprehension is not my purpose.

Clearly, they're all on edge. Walking a thin line between sanity and insanity. How much horror can their mortal minds witness before they fall into madness? Humanity. What a creation! I've always seen them as some kind of odd gamble, but at times I see how it's paid off.

They have the pure potential of Divine power, but also the power of the purely infernal inside them. Give them free will and the game is begun. Now that we're at the end of this iteration of the game, the final questions are being answered.

Will they rise above, or will they fall?

I know they will never see it. They can't possibly comprehend the depths of the game, but a game it is. Or at least that's the best analogy to it. In the Rapture, the best of them were removed, those who had demonstrated greater Divine tendencies than Infernal without any doubt.

These who remained were those who hadn't chosen a path yet. Their decisions had not left them in the clear-cut good or bad. Even these beings the Divine loves. I feel its love flowing through, even as I perceive the horrors of the war. Even as I have committed atrocities by its will, the atrocities are done with love.

Then there is Aviella.

She is... pure. Simple, perfect, and separate from everything, yet interwoven with it all. My guts tighten, my heart races, and my mouth goes dry thinking of her. Her love rivals that of the Divine. Her ability to forgive. To find the good in all that she sees, no matter who or what it is, is stunning.

She saved Tynan, Alaric, and Shen. The Horsemen, creatures with a single, infernal purpose, but she saw the men in them. She pulled them back from the Shadow. A feat I would never have believed if I hadn't seen and felt it.

She changed the game. Overturned the table and set down a new board.

Soon it will be time. Soon I will give myself to her, willingly, because there is nothing better than her, and I will give all to her.

"Would you stop staring at me!" a man yells, jerking my attention.

"I would but you're so damn ugly," another man says.

"Hey, he's not as ugly as you, you son-of-a-bitch!" a third man enters the fray.

Three. Something oppressive wafts through the air, a hint of Shadow with the deftest of touches. This is it.

A half-dozen other passengers near them move quickly away as the three men devolve into an all-out brawl. The demon is racing closer, his magic pulsing against mine, coming to my aid.

"Stop!" I order, willing them to obey.

Two of them glance in my direction but their eyes are filled with rage. Rage so hot it burns past the magic behind my command. The rage of freewill corrupted. One of them grins, shakes his head, then swings at another.

I leap over retreating passengers so I can dive forward to tackle him. Pain. White hot, bursting stars in my vision, as something stabs into my stomach. The stars give way to a burning, raging fire emanating from the source.

"Nate!" Rafe yells, as he enters the train.

I can't tear my eyes away from the knife sticking out of my guts. It's pulling my magic as if it's drinking it. The three fighting men knock into me, and I'm taken off my feet, slamming against the floor with two of them wrestling on top of me.

The air is knocked out of my lungs and the knife is driven deeper. I reach deep to draw on the Eternal Flame, wrapping it around me like a cloak. The pain pushes back, staying outside the protective layer. My thoughts clear. A fist slams into my face but it's a distant thing.

Rafe appears past the fighting men on top of me, grabs one of them by the back of his shirt and lifts him off me easily. He tosses the man to one side then grabs the next.

Blood covers my shirt and pools around me. I climb to my feet, one hand hovering protectively over the blade piercing my guts. I'm careful, trying to not cause further internal damage. Numbness spreads from that entry point as it continues to feed on my magic. It's growing stronger.

"Rafe..." I gasp, the world tilting around me.

Desperate, I grab the back of a bench, holding myself upright through power of will.

"STOP!" Rafe yells, his voice echoing on itself.

His eyes are full black, and his aura is outlined in black flames as he draws his magic close. The three men freeze in place, unable to move against the power of the demon's magic. Rage contorts his face. He's struggling against the dark nature of his magic. Holding back the pure destruction it demands he unleash.

Impossibly one of the men moves, slowly and obviously painfully, but his hand balls into a fist as he turns to the demon.

That can't be. No human possesses that much power. Suddenly the air is too heavy. Too thick to breathe. Weighted as if the molecules are ten thousand times thicker. Rafe and I lock eyes, and I see the recognition in his.

"Shit—"

"DEATH MAGIC!" Silas yells, cutting off Rafe before he finishes.

CHAPTER NINETEEN

RAFE

*S*ilas slams the door to one side and enters the train car in a single motion.

"DEATH MAGIC!" he yells, cutting into my own curse of it.

Death magic, the darkest, worst of magic. It's not even destruction. Death magic is annihilation. It's erasing all that is and all that was. It's the blackest of voids possible. A coldness sweeps over my skin. Nate is hurt, badly it seems, but I don't have time to help him.

If the Shadow is bringing death magic to bear, then this is it. An end-game move. A tinge of regret flickers inside, as I know what I have to do. I'm not sure I'll pull this off, but I have to try.

Opening myself up I reach out, magically, and pull the ambient magic to me. The ambient magic of Wormwood.

Dark, twisted, infernal, and full of evil intent. I drink of it deep, and when I'm full to brimming, my eyes burning, limbs trembling, bile boiling up my throat, I pull yet more.

It's been millennia since I've pulled in so much power.

More than I can contain, more than I can possibly handle, but I must do this.

The passengers around us scream, covering their ears, and ducking their heads. Blood drips from their eyes and seeps out from under their hands.

I have to save them. For her.

Somehow.

Drawing deeper, the power washes through...

CHAPTER TWENTY

AVIELLA

erking, I'm awake. Rolling off of Efram, I barely get my head stuck into the walkway before retching. I'm feverish, burning up, my stomach clenches tight forcing its contents burning up my throat. Tears fill my eyes.

"Avi," Efram says, shifting to hold my hair for me.

It won't stop. Revulsion. My magic recoils from whatever it is. The stench of decay fills my nostrils, my vision swims, and I can't stop my stomach rebelling. Gagging, I struggle to bring myself under control but the nausea comes in waves.

It's the magic. Something foul and nasty that keeps hitting me in wave after wave. It's assaulting my senses on both a physical and metaphysical level. Even though I'm trembling, I push myself upright, biting down hard to stop my stomach from expelling more.

Weakly, I trace symbols in the air. It's taking all my effort to keep my hands up and making the motions. Soft glowing lines form in the air then fade away as the shield goes into effect.

Instantly I feel better. The nausea is gone leaving weakness in its wake, but at least I'm not holding back retching.

"What in the nine hells was that?" I pull out of Efram's arms and climb out of the bench seat.

"I don't know," he says. "But I think—"

A force wave slams into both of us, and I'm knocked off my feet. The air is knocked out of my lungs when I land flat on my back. Gasping, I climb back to my feet, anger rising as I do.

"Damn it," I curse. "This stops. Now."

"Avi," Efram says as he unentangles himself from the bench and table we'd been sitting at.

I ignore him and storm down the path toward the next car. The force came from that direction, and the magic is strongest this way. Something is pulling power, a lot of it, creating a sick green glowing beacon in my magical sight.

Whatever it is, it's going to regret fucking with me. Today is not the day.

When I step between the cars, I notice that the air rushing past and even the noise of the cars clacking down the rail are oddly suppressed. As if some kind of dampener lies over us. The land feels... empty. It's one of those background things you quickly grow accustomed to, but now it feels like all the latent magic of the area is gone. Drained.

Through the window of the door to the next car the lights flicker, intermixing with a darkness that is at odds with the weak sunlight which should illuminate the space. When I grab the handle of the door, green flames spark to life and trail up my arm. My own magic consumes it, using the infernal magic to fuel itself.

My anger burns hotter, and my lips curl into a grimace. Something is messing with us, and I've had enough. I'm ready to strike back.

With the door open, I get my first full view of the chaos.

Directly in my path is Silas, on his knees and straining to rise. His magic has formed a protective shell around him. Darkness presses against the shell, forcing him further down. Sweat pours down his face as he struggles against the powerful magic.

It's a new magic, tasting of endless darkness with a stench of final despair. The air is filled with the odor of grave dirt and maggots. Decay assaults my nose.

In the center of the car, outlined with a putrid green glow, is Rafe. He smiles when he sees me, his grin going from ear to ear but there is no mirth on his face. His eyes are pure black, and in the pupils burn the infernal fires.

"Hey, Aviella,' he says, his voice casual. "Glad you could come."

He's talking through gritted teeth. His clenched fists move in circles over his head as he pulls in power. The more he pulls, the brighter he glows in my magic sight.

"Rafe," I say.

"You should stand back, doll," he says, squaring his shoulders.

Blackness roils through the car. The survivors are screaming, hands over their ears, blood streaming from between their fingers and out of their eyes.

"Rafe, let me—"

His smile cuts me off. It's vicious and loving and filled with pain all at the same time.

"Not this time, kiddo," he says, sweat pouring down his face with hints of red in it. "Let the bad guy be bad."

"You're not bad," I say, heart leaping into my throat.

"I'm the worst," he says. "You only see... the good... in me."

"I do," I say, and it's an oath. It rings with magic as I say it.

The darkness roiling around us blocks out everything and everyone but him and me. He's drawn in the ambient magic of Wormwood. Infernal tainted magic, which he's using as fuel to fight the darkness. I'd never have thought there'd be dark magic that was worse than the infernal magic.

"Aviella," he growls. "Get out."

"No," I say, shaking my head.

I can't lose him. The outline of him is blurring, fuzzy, as if he's being torn apart in front of my eyes, molecule by molecule.

"Can't hold this long," he says. "I'm sorry, I have to do this. Have to save them…. For you."

My heart breaks as tears stream down my face.

"Don't do this, Rafe," I say, magic swelling inside of me.

I reach out and pull more magic. Grabbing it from everywhere I can. Latent potential from the survivors, ancient Methuselah magic from Silas, angelic power from Nate. I meld it into one, form it into a shield, a weapon against the pressing death around us.

It's not enough. I need more. Magically, I cry out to the universe, to anyone who can help. I stretch for Tynan, Alaric, and Shen, but I can't seem to reach them. They're not there when I call.

Something pops behind me, and the scent of burning incense fills the air. I can't take time to turn around, but I don't sense danger. I'm molding magic around Rafe, holding his form together, trying to keep him from dispersing into… I don't know.

"Aviella," Gavin says, appearing next to me.

He places a hand on the small of my back and I latch onto his magic, drawing it into me. He gasps in surprise. It powers me but still I need more.

I reach out and find Killian, then Ronan. The mages are

clean, pure magic. Human magic, different than all the others. I drink it from them, hearing their yelps of surprise, but I don't have time. I have to save Rafe.

"Aviella, don't!" Rafe yells. "Damn it, girl, let me do my part!"

"I'm not losing you," I swear.

Sweat pours down my face, dripping into my eyes. Weaving my hands, I trace angelic symbols in the air around Rafe, forming a protective shield. His black eyes lock on me, and we glare at each other. He pushes out the power he's pulled in, so much power I can't believe he's holding it together at all.

It's coming off of him in waves, pushing against the oppressive death magic threatening us all. Death pushes back, stronger. It's a tsunami of blackness swelling higher and higher as it swamps over us.

The mages struggle to remain upright. Gavin is holding onto a bench, staring at me with wide eyes. He shakes his head negative, but I can't stop. Saving Rafe is what matters.

"I'm sorry," I whisper, drawing more of their power into me.

The three mages drop to their knees crying out in pain. Silas screams and distantly I hear Nate gasp, more in my head than with my ears.

I take all they have to offer, drinking deeply of them, and pool it with my magic. The buzz becomes thunder, a storm ready to unleash. I walk forward, tingles racing over my skin, hair rising around my head as I move closer to Rafe.

Death pushes against me. A building pressure, escalating higher and higher. The force behind the opposing magic fights, pushing against me. When I try to take a step the air itself resists me, forming a barrier between Rafe and me.

Decay, rot, and behind it all, emptiness. Black, empty, nothingness presses in, laying claim to the world around us.

Reaching for Rafe. If that touches him, I'll lose him. Forever. I know it beyond the shadow of a doubt. He'll be gone, with no hope of return.

Resolve finds new depths to my magic. A memory flits past my thoughts, both distracting and empowering. I recall lying on a stiff bed in some cheap hotel eating fast food and watching tv. The mouse dressed as a sorcerer standing on a rocky promontory, conducting the symphony of the storm.

"You see that Avi?" Dad asks, his voice warmth itself.

"Yeah," I say, awe in my voice.

"That can be you, baby," he says. "You're special. Don't you ever forget it. You're going to be the one Avi."

"Really?" seven-year-old me asked.

"Have I ever lied to you?" he asks, a grin on his face.

Conducting the storm, like a symphony. Something about that memory strikes a chord, and there's a shift inside of me. Suddenly I understand. I'm not conducting my magic, I'm wrestling it. If I do this...

The air around me sparks blue-purple, and there's the scent of ozone. That fresh smell after a thunderstorm has washed the earth. It's clean and a welcome relief from the stench of death.

"Avi?" Rafe asks, his eyes widening.

It's my turn. I grin at him and nod. The blurring outline of his body solidifies as I direct my power around him, embracing his form carefully so as to not overwhelm him. Relief fills his face, and then his power calls to me too. I draw it in and ease off the others. They gasp almost as one, and around me I sense rather than see them rising to their feet.

As I gather them to me, I feel the dragons now. They're far away and busy, but their power is mine to use as I need it. All my men. Killian, Gavin, Ronan, Luca, Silas, Efram, Nate, Rafe, the three dragons... but something is missing. An empty ache in my space where I know, instinctively there should be something. It's that sensation you have when you've lost a tooth and you are acutely aware of the emptiness where something should be.

It's enough though. Their power flows to me, through me, as I conduct and direct it. Swirling it together with flourishes of my arms and focusing it into symbols of power. New symbols, ones I've not been taught but I know they're right.

Weaving the symbols of magic around us, I form a shield, then push it out. The death magic presses in, increasing its pressure, something pouring more force into it, but I'm in my element. I'm fire and I'm wind, joining to make a blaze that will not be extinguished.

I scream a battle cry, and, thrusting my hands out, I explode the magic away. It detonates outward and the death magic is shattered, broken into millions of pieces. It rains around us and dissipates into nothingness.

My vision is swimming. Three Rafes approach, each one wearing his trademarked boyish grin, three smiling faces dance around, then I'm falling...

CHAPTER TWENTY-ONE

GAVIN

"*H*ow is she?" Silas asks, trying to rise from the table again.

Luca pushes him back down and readjusts the Atlantean Crystal hanging over him to assess any damage to his magic.

"She's fine," I say. "Worry about you, old man."

Aviella lies on another table, unconscious, yet still beautiful. She's beautiful in ways that a girl shouldn't be able to be because it's not physical, at least not only. She positively glows in my magic sight, and that glow transfers to her on this plane too.

We collect, train, and save Innocents. I would never have thought there could be something like her. Something that would surprise me after all these years. My brothers and I, our journey through time has been long, and the world has changed even before the Apocalypse. The weight of the ages weighs heavily.

"Yes," Silas says. "I'm older than all of you put together. So let me do my damn job, I know when I'm fine or not."

"Silas," Luca says. "Let us help. She damn near drained

you. We can help recharge your magical pools, and you know it. You're worried about her and about the attack."

Silas stops fighting, dropping his head back down on the table with a thud.

"Fine," he says.

Luca re-centers the crystal and activates it again. It pulses blood red, emitting a soft, healing power into Silas. He'll be fine. The Methuselah almost always is. Almost.

Aviella stirs, and my attention shifts back to her. I'm in the middle of crafting new wards around her which would be a lot easier if she slept longer, but it doesn't look like I'm going to have a choice. Her eyelids flutter, her lips part, and I'm struck by the fullness of them. The desire to taste them is almost more than I can resist.

"Rafe!" she yells, sitting straight up and sucking almost all the magic out of the room.

It takes us all by surprise. Luca and Silas yelp and I'm dropped to my knees.

"Aviella!" I yell. She looks around wild-eyed, not fully awake and here. "It's over!"

She raises her hands, magic forming a bright, white ball between them that's tinged with blue. She blinks rapidly, breathing in ragged gasps. The soft spot at the base of her throat shows that her heart is racing. I touch the calf of her leg and push soothing magic into her.

Her breathing eases, her heart slows, and she lets the magic go. I get up, lean against the table, and let my head clear. Damn, she's becoming more powerful than even we expected. And she's not done yet. There's one more for her to add to our harem before the prophecies will be fulfilled. Only then will she fully awaken the goddess inside of her.

"Sorry," she says, one hand going to her head as her brow furrows in pain. "Damn."

"You okay?" I ask.

"My head is splitting. Do we have any aspirin?" she asks.

"I'll see if we can find some," I offer. "May I?"

Because of her volatility, I ask before I touch her. She looks at me through her fingers, then nods her assent. I place my fingers on her temples and let my magic flow into her, seeking out her pain and numbing it. She shivers then relaxes, her hand dropping to her side.

"Thanks," she says. She opens her eyes slowly, as if testing her vision, and looks around. "Silas, you okay?"

"I'm fine," he says. "As soon as these thrice-cursed Templars finish their playing around, I'll be able to do my work."

"Luckily, there's four of us," Luca says. "So you didn't curse all of us."

"I know," Silas growls.

The crystal pulses over him still, but it softens and then turns dull. Luca grabs the crystal from where it is floating over the Methuselah.

"There, all done," he says.

"Good," Silas says, all but leaping to his feet. "I've work to do. Aviella, if you need me, call."

He doesn't bother with further goodbyes, leaving the storage area we're working in. The clatter of the train grows louder when he opens the door then dampens once more as he leaves. Aviella is gripping the edges of the table so hard her knuckles are turning white. She's trying to hide how drained she is, but I sense it.

It's admirable. She's being 'strong' the best way she knows how. I could call her on it, but it would serve no purpose. I'll let her grow. She's finding her feet and coming to terms with what she's meant to be. It does no good for me to interfere with that.

"How long?" she asks, her voice rough, almost a croak.

"Couple of hours," I answer, understanding her question.

"Rafe?" she asks.

"He's fine," I say.

"You're sure?" she asks, fixing me with a piercing gaze as her magic gathers, weighing the truth of my words.

"I am," I say, feeling the resonance of truth as I say it. "He's... well, meditating is the best way to describe it. He's healing the magical pathways that he strained pulling all that power in."

"He's a damn fool," she mutters. "I almost lost him."

"Yes," I agree.

Luca comes over and takes a seat next to her. He's casual, at-ease with her, and she seems to be the same. A fast stab of jealousy hits me, but I push it away. What do I have to be jealous of? This is our fate. I've known it since we found her.

She is not meant for one of us alone. In our own way, we are but keys. Keys to unlock her full potential. Acceptance of that role is the only way forward. The fate of the world, literally, hangs in the balance. Still, no matter how rational I am, no matter how deep I bury the feeling, it's there. The way she looks at him as he lays a gentle hand on top of hers.

"We're adding some wards to you," I say, forcing my thoughts out of the spiral that jealousy threatens to create.

"Sure," she exhales, relaxing a little.

"They'll help you to channel more power," Luca says.

She turns towards him and smiles. She's pale, waxen almost, but her smile is still brilliant as the sun. She's breathing heavily, causing her chest to rise and fall, and I can't help my attention going to it.

"Just what I need," she says, leaning into Luca.

She rests her head on his shoulder. A vulnerable moment. My hands itch, urging me to touch her, so I give in to it. I touch her shoulder blade. The tension forms hard knots in her muscles. Gently I massage and she groans.

"Relax," I say. "We're here. You're safe."

"For now," she exhales into Luca's chest.

His stormy eyes meet mine with an inquiring look. The fire burning in them, the burning need he's feeling is a mirror for my own. Aviella reaches up, touches his face as she raises her head, running her fingers through his blonde beard.

She pulls him close and kisses him.

My cock is instantly, painfully hard. Straining against the restraint of my pants, demanding to be free. As I run my fingers over her back, her knotted muscles ease as she deepens the kiss. Luca's arms wrap around her, trailing down her sides. She moans into their kiss.

She breaks the kiss, turning towards me, reaching out. She hooks my neck and pulls me into the sweetest heaven I've ever dreamed of. Her lips on mine are soft, lush, the touch of perfection on my skin. Magic swirls in bright colors around the three of us.

She parts my lips and unbuttons her shirt. I can't tear my eyes away, watching as she reveals creamy, smooth skin until her breasts are bare, heaving in and out with each breath. My mouth waters, my cock throbs, and I want nothing more than to touch her, to taste her.

She hooks her arm around my neck and around Luca at the same time. She pulls us in, placing us each on one of her breasts.

I follow her lead, taking her nipple in my mouth, rolling it over with my tongue. Letting my hands roam across her body. She gasps her pleasure, pushing her chest forward, demanding more.

"Yes," she growls.

I am clay in her hands. The magic dancing around us is a net, pulling us together, binding the three of us together. Exploring her body is a delight, but the motions weave a spell. Luca and I are woven into her, the fabric of what she's becoming.

She draws on our magic, sucking it in even as she takes in our breath with each kiss. Each touch adds to the sigils to bind us all. It's not only us, we're part of the greater whole. Woven together with the others.

Memories flash rapid fire as excitement builds.

She undoes my pants, then Luca's, our cocks bouncing free, and she gives them each equal attention. There is no jealousy in this loving, there is a perfect balance, and in the end our focus is her. The pleasure we take is not for our flesh, but hers.

I recall the beginning. Trudging through the desert heat to a tower that stood in two planes at once. Entering the Sacred Temple where I swore myself to our cause. To protect the Innocents. To stand against the Shadow. To serve through the end of time.

I didn't know then that the end would ever come.

I didn't know then what pleasures I would know in the end.

Her mouth is hot, wet, and a delight of sensual pleasure. Her body is revealed in stages, each part new, beautiful, a feast for the eyes.

She kneels between us and gives us pleasure, but as she does, she pulls our magic into her along with our bodies. The physical connection makes the transfer smooth.

I feel my magic swirling in her now, joining with her on the second plane, becoming part of her and strengthening our connection. I'm about to explode, physically and meta-physically both. We're dancing on the edge.

She moves with the grace of a ballerina, guiding us along the edge of the stage without a single slip. She rises between us, gripping both of our cocks, guiding us to face her.

"Mine," she whispers, magic resonating with the word.

"Yours," we intone together, completing the ritual.

I give myself freely to her, and I know that Luca does the same. We've known, for a long time, this was to be our fate. We've known that she would come. And we've waited, ready to serve, and through her, serve the Divine.

She is the one hope we have. Without her the world will fall to the Shadow. With her, we stand a chance.

She wiggles out of her pants and climbs back onto the table, positioning herself to take us fully. She pushes me around so that I'm between her legs and guides Luca towards her head. I'm placed at her opening, ready to enter, but I hold back. Teasing myself with what is to come, clearing my head so I can fully appreciate it.

Luca guides himself into her mouth, and the sounds of her moaning pleasure and his gasps as she does is almost enough to push me over. My cock jumps and leaks begging for its release.

Unhurriedly, I slide into her. It's a warm grip that focuses all my thoughts and attention onto her and the connection between us.

Magic swells surging as our bodies come together. Joining on a spiritual level as the three of us find our pleasures. Her moans and sighs reward our attention. I will give all I am for her.

Thrusting in she takes, learning, her magic passing through my memories as she gains, innately, the understandings it's taken me lifetimes to acquire. She absorbs the knowledge.

The physical is so much less, a cheap mockery of what is happening in my magic. I switch with Luca, unspoken, responding to her desires. The pleasure builds until it's all I can do to hold back, to not fall over to my desperately desired release.

Her soft skin glows in my sight. She's outlined in golden

light, a light so pure it burns but attracts, it heals even as it destroys. It burns away uncertainty and forges from its shattered parts something new. Hope.

She replaces all she takes with a renewal of desire. Belief that we can succeed. Her power is awe-inspiring, and in it I find comfort. She takes me into her mouth, and then her body arches. All of our magic swells, swirling to incredible heights, and then as one we explode with her.

Even through my release I'm aware of her, her pleasure, her beauty, but most of all her purity. In this brief moment we've pushed back the darkness but as I let myself go, I see the lines of fate twisting out before her, and ahead is a turning point.

A betrayal will happen. It's brief, too brief for me to see clearly. Someone will betray her, and beyond that point her fate line ends. The future beyond that is clouded in shadow. She's in more danger than we know.

I have to tell the others....

CHAPTER TWENTY-TWO

AVIELLA

J collapse into the orgasm, letting it take me and cleanse away the stench of death that clings to my magic. Drawing in their magic helps me to understand them, to know them better than I did before. The mages are less mysterious now.

I'm recharged. The fight against that death magic, my need to save Rafe, drained more than I realized. I'd felt empty to the point I wasn't sure I could wield magic any longer. Definitely not something I was going to share with the guys. I know how they'd freak out.

Luca peppers me with sweet, soft kisses as Gavin runs his fingers through my hair. I bask in their attention while letting the magic flow through me. Gavin discreetly draws fresh protective wards around me, and I have to wonder if he thinks I don't notice. Since it doesn't really matter, I'm going to let him think he's being clever.

Someone knocks on the door, interrupting our afterglow.

"Gavin, Luca," Killian calls out.

He must know what we're doing in here because he doesn't open the door. Normally I'd expect him to barge in.

The mages have a penchant for appearing at the right moment. The boys look at each other before answering.

"Yeah," Luca says.

"Wrap up," he orders, and then his footsteps recede.

Gavin laughs before grabbing his clothes and starting to dress. I take the moment to admire his body while he does, drifting my attention between him and Luca. Old scars mar his muscled form. Some of them bring memories to mind, part of my joining with him I suppose. I know how he got the scars, even feeling shadows of the pain that came with them.

"We need to put more wards around you," Luca says.

"More than you were?" I ask, grinning mischievously.

It's obvious from the way they look at each other that they didn't know I realized that they were trying to put them on me without my awareness.

Luca has the decency to look abashed at being called out, but he nods firmly. "Yes."

"Okay," I agree. "Why did you guys show up? Not that I'm not grateful."

I add the last as I grab my own clothes and dress.

"We felt your need," Gavin says. "Knew something was up, if not what."

"Glad you did," I say.

I'm not sure I could have beat the shadow's attack without their extra reserves to pull from.

Gavin nods, seriousness settling on his face.

"It's going to get more dangerous," he says. "They're not going to pull punches any longer."

"You mean to say they have been?" I ask, anger and fear forming a weird mix that leaves my stomach roiling.

"Aviella," Luca says, placing a warm hand on the small of my back.

"What?" I ask, rage rising over the fear. "I almost lost

Rafe! He was sacrificing himself, to save me. We lost.... So many of the passengers I can't even count their bodies, much less know their names. Bunker after bunker has fallen. Everywhere I go is death and destruction!"

"We know," the two mages say as one. "It's not over, Aviella."

I'm shaking so hard. My hands are balled into fists so tight that my nails dig into the palms. My heart pounds like a machine-gun and magic fills the room, dancing along with my emotions. I slow my breathing, and steeling my control, I close my eyes.

Images dance behind my eyes, memories that aren't mine. The two mages dressed as knights, clanking as they walk through stone halls. Their despair is palpable, the acrid scent of burning flesh fills their nostrils. Shaking my head, I push that aside and focus my thoughts into the now.

"This is your destiny," Gavin says. "I don't say fate, fate would mean there's a pre-set outcome. There's not. Luca and I, we've been on the edge before. We thought the world had ended once before but now we know it was only to prepare us for this moment."

"What does that even mean, Gavin?" I snap. "How the hell is that supposed to make it any better. We're losing more than we're gaining."

Gavin grips my shoulders. "I know how hard this is."

He stares into my eyes, holding me with his steely gaze. The memory tugs, pulling me into their past, and it is theirs, not mine. I know it and I see in his face he knows it too.

"I have to stop them," I say, anger bleeding away.

"We will," he says.

I pull my pants the rest of the way on and finish dressing. The boys are dressed and we're presentable to show the world again. Killian and the rest wait for us outside, and it's time to keep this show rolling forward.

We gather around the table again. It feels more complete to have the mages here. When we enter the dining car, Ronan looks up from his conversation with Silas. His eyes are assessing, weighing me, or scanning. He smiles, a half smile that's sexy as hell.

"Food's ready," Efram says, laying out another steaming bag.

We dig in with soft conversation. Mostly it's dominated by an avoidance of what we're facing. No one offers anything of import while we take our food. When that part of the meal is over Efram pours coffee for each of us.

"The train is almost to the next bunker," Silas says. "We need to be in tight coordination."

"About what? Anyone know what we'll be facing inside there?" I ask.

"We need you to investigate rumors of Innocents there," Ronan says.

"Can't you detect them?" I ask.

"Yes, normally," Ronan says.

"Something is blocking our ability to scan there," Killian say. "It's affecting the astral planes all around the area."

"Weird," I observe.

"Maybe Luca and Gavin could do a 'special' investigation with Avi," Rafe says, leaning way back in his chair with a boyish grin, his eyes darting between Luca, Gavin, and me.

It's almost as if he knows. My cheeks warm and his grin widens.

"That's what we know," Ronan continues, picking up where Killian left off, ignoring Rafe who chuckles deep in his throat making me blush more.

I hide my face behind the coffee cup wishing the demon would shut up.

"We can look but it's going to be hard," Nate says. "Once

we're inside, we'll have to play within the rules of their system."

"Rules are made to be broken, my friend," Rafe offers.

"Rafe, you know better," Nate says.

"Sure," he says. "You're a party pooper."

"I'm going to stay with you," Luca says.

"You are? What about the rest of you?" I ask, surprised by the offer.

"We can't join you, yet," Ronan says. "But we want to make sure you have extra eyes on your back while you're in there."

"Any word on my Dad?" I ask. "Have you detected anything?"

"No," Killian says.

"I'm sure he's there," I say with more confidence than I'm feeling.

"I'll help," Luca says.

"Okay," I say, pushing away from the table. "I'm going to check on the passengers."

"Aviella," Silas says. "Do you feel ready?"

I stop mid-stride and stare at my mentor. It's a serious question, one none of them have really asked me. What chance have I had to be 'ready'? My life has been one situation after the next thrust onto me, ready or not.

"Yes," I say, turning to face the table. "Together, we'll stand or we'll fall, but it will be together."

Efram smiles, rises from the table, and comes over to me. The rest of my men nod their agreement, though everyone but Rafe looks grim. Turning my back on them I step out of the car and then cross the gap to the next one. Efram follows behind me silently.

"Avi," he says, his voice soft and warm, like a fuzzy blanket that I want to curl up in and forget the world outside.

"Yeah," I say, glancing over my shoulder.

No matter how much I want to stop and cuddle up, I've got to check on these passengers.

"Are you okay?" he asks.

"Yeah," I say, climbing around a pile of crates.

I stop and take a seat on one of them. Efram sits next to me. The silence that falls is comfortable, but my thoughts aren't. He puts an arm around my shoulders, and I lay my head against him. The train rattles its way down the track but nothing else disturbs the moment.

"Efram?" I ask at last.

"Yeah?"

"It's going to get bad," I say, trying to put the feelings I have into words.

"Yes," he agrees.

"I may need..." I don't know how to say or ask what I know I need to. I'm not sure why even. "I need someone I can count on. Someone I know, no matter what, will do what needs to be done."

"Like what, Avi?"

"I don't know," I say, somberly.

"Did one of the guys... do something?" he asks.

"No," I shake my head. "No, but they all... have their ideas, goals, and I need someone who... doesn't."

"I have my own ideas," he says, but his voice is soft and filled with understanding.

"I know," I sigh. "I'm not saying this right. Just... be you, Efram. Please, just be you."

"I will," he says, squeezing me tight. "I'm here for you. I'll do what you think is best."

"No matter what?" I ask, and as I do magic surges around us causing him to pause.

"Avi..." he trails off, but I wait, biting my lip. "Yes."

The magic tingles across our skin as he agrees.

CHAPTER TWENTY-THREE

AVIELLA

"*W*ill they accept us there?" a frightened girl in her early twenties asks.

"I don't honestly know," I say.

I'm sitting in one of the booth-like chairs. The surviving twenty-one passengers have arrayed themselves around the car, peppering me with questions.

"I heard they don't like make-up," another girl asks.

"Or skinny people," a guy adds.

"Or fat people," someone else chimes in.

"Listen," I say. "I can't answer most of your questions. "Truth is, I don't know. All we can do is survive."

"Survive," they murmur in soft unison as if that single word has some power of its own.

"How?" an older man asks. "How do we keep surviving? They took out Tynan's bunker. He's a dragon, for god's sake! What hope do we have?"

When I meet his gaze, it's easy to see the terror written clearly on his face. More than seeing it, it washes over me. As it's joined by the others on the car it's almost enough to pull me under, but something rumbles inside my magic, and then their negative emotions lighten. As they do, a burst of fresh energy rushes through me like the first taste of black coffee.

"We have hope," I say firmly. "We make hope. It's on us to survive, but more than that, we have to become better."

"Better?" someone asks.

"Yes, better," I say. "Don't be petty, don't be jealous. Be better. Help one anoth—"

Suddenly it feels like the inside of my head explodes with pain and noise. A tingling sensation races around it and down my back and spine. Something screams, grabbing my attention and I see a blur ahead of the train.

"What is it?" one of the survivors asks but I can't see them.

"Buckle in," I order, leaping to my feet.

My head keeps pounding as I run down the train car, and it sounds like birds are screeching inside my skull.

"Rafe, Nate!" I yell, stumbling into the dining car.

"Avi?" Nate is at my side, taking me in his arms but there's no time. We're in danger and must act fast.

"Outside," I order, pointing.

"What is—" he starts.

"No, ahead, trouble, go! In the air now!" I bark the order.

Nate doesn't hesitate any longer. He leaps backwards, spreads his wings, and flies up.

"Rafe, help him," I bark.

The confusion on his face doesn't stop him from moving. He jumps up, grabbing the edge of the next car's roof, then scrambles over the top and disappears.

"Shit," his curse comes back over the whipping wind.

The mages aren't waiting for orders. One after another they pop and disappear, teleporting into the danger, leaving Efram and me alone.

"Protect the passengers," I say, grabbing his hands and squeezing them tight.

"Got it," he says moving past me to their car.

The screeching in my head hasn't stopped, but it's not as loud. It's trying to tell me something, but I don't speak bird screech. My skin tingles as my magic ebbs and flows around me, swelling then retreating, waiting for me to channel it.

I grab the ladder and climb up onto the roof with Rafe. The wind whips my hair into my face as I climb over the top, and I have to stop to push it away. Rafe is already two cars ahead, pulsing with the red-black of his magic.

A fresh monstrosity is standing past Rafe to the right of the track, staring at the approaching train. It looks like a wooly mammoth that died, came back, died again, and was raised once more. It's massive, as big as one of the train cars, with long curling tusks that are broken off to jagged edges. Its fur is dirty and matted. It looks like something has taken massive bites out of its hide, and where the old wounds are the flesh is rotting and black. Worse, the wounds look like they're moving of their own accord. It faces the train and stares it down with huge red eyes that gleam in the dim light. It raises its trunk and sounds its challenge.

It's obvious what it intends to do. The mammoth-monster is going to charge the intruder that's challenging its territory. I've no doubt this is another Wormwood experiment gone wrong. I know the government was experimenting with cloning, but this is worse than I'd imagined.

Nate hovers in the sky over it. He pulls out a flaming sword, and Rafe is running across the train cars towards it, drawing a blazing black sword of his own. I move to run towards Rafe so I can help when the screeching in my head reaches a crescendo, and instead I drop to my knees, holding my head in both hands to keep it from exploding.

The sound is deafening, even if it's only in my head. Clenching my teeth doesn't help. I pull magic protectively around myself, pushing the sound back. Now it passes through a wall before reaching me and then it changes. It's not screeching, its words.

We're coming.

Who's coming? The pain is receding. I open my eyes and scan the area for who or what is coming. It must be some new threat. Who or what else would be coming?

I assume this monster mammoth thing is bad luck, but if something else is going to attack us at the same time, that's a plan. A bad plan, for us.

I leap to my feet and run down the train car. A touch of magic makes me sure footed—each step I take sticks to the roof so I don't slip or fall despite the wind pushing me one way, then another. All my hours of training are paying off.

"Rafe!" I yell as I get close enough to have a chance of being heard. "More trouble. Something is—"

Nate yells something jerking my attention up. A black cloud drops out of the sky, diving at us. I weave my hands and a golden shield appears above us, dancing with magical sigils etched in silver. It's big enough to cover the entire car. By stretching to my limit, I am able to include Rafe.

The black cloud takes shape as it comes closer. It's a flock of birdmen. More Wormwood experiments, I'm certain, some infernal, evil crossing of genetics. They're each a full-sized man, male bodies, but their arms are wings, with hands at the end of them inside the feathers. Their feet are claws, like that of a bird of prey. They're creepy, especially as they dive bomb towards us.

They screech, loud, and it echoes the screeching in my head. They dive past Nate in an impressive display of aerial acrobatics to avoid his flaming sword. He performs his own impressive display as he gives chase. They're heading for my shield, right at Rafe.

I pour power into the shield and brace for the impact

about to happen. They turn at the last instant, twirling in the air and attacking the mammoth.

Their taloned feet tear at it, one after another, as they dive in then fly out. The flock of them are tearing away chunks of rotting flesh with each pass.

The mammoth bellows in pain, adding more sound to the cacophony of the screeching from the bird men.

One of the birdmen breaks from the flock. He's bigger than the others. If he was a normal man, I'd guess he'd be seven feet tall and muscular. His nose is long and sharp, beak-like without being a beak. He hovers in the air moving down to be on an eye level with me, while remaining outside my shield.

He smiles, showing rows of sharp pointy teeth that do not belong in the mouth of a man or man-looking thing. It makes my blood run cold, but there's no malice behind the smile.

He narrows his eyes, concentrating. My head tingles. Beyond the magic is the screeching that almost sounds like words.

Concentrating myself I focus on the sound, trying to understand it.

Suddenly, it's clear. It's him. He's talking to me. As I focus, the thrill of my magic lights up my nerves, and I shiver as the screeching resolves into words again, but now it's easier to understand than it was. I'm no longer hearing the screeching and pulling words out of it, I understand him.

We help.

"Shit," I exhale.

Rafe lands next to me with a thud, startling me.

"What is happening?" he asks, positioning himself a step in front of me with his sword held across his body.

"It's talking to me," I say, shaking my head in disbelief.

"Well," Rafe says. "Oh hell, why not. Anything good?"

He gives me a fast flash of his grin before returning his full attention to the birdman.

"They're helping," I say.

Images press against me, so I ease my shield, only a little, and accept them. I almost wish I hadn't.

The cold, uncaring experiments that were done to create these creatures. They were torturing children with a specific genetic mutation. One that made it possible for them to bind their DNA to that of other creatures.

I see it all, and it leaves me sick, my knees weak and shaking. Bile rises in my throat as I understand what humans have done. The horror of it is almost more than I can bear.

Behind the horror rises anger.

People did this. Evil people. People who do not deserve to be saved, they deserve punishment. Pulling power in fuels my rage. I want to destroy the ones who did this.

No.

The simple thought cuts through my rage.

"How can you say no?" I yell at the birdman. "They did this to you! They tortured you!"

Yes.

Yes. He knows, he agrees, but in his thoughts is forgiveness. More images come through. They've made themselves a tribe. They're families, caring for each other, protecting one another. They don't harbor malice or hate. They don't allow room for that in their lives.

Warmth replaces the burn of the anger. A soothing warmth. What happened to them is wrong, but as he flows his feelings to me, it becomes clear that they've forgiven the past. They accept the sacrifices they've made. There is the now and the future.

It's a lesson I need too. I can't save those I've lost. There's a price for everything we do, and someone has to pay it.

Something tugs at me, deep inside, pulling me towards....

147

I don't know. The mammoth turns and stomps away as the birdmen continue attacking it until it runs over a hill and out of sight. They return and hover in the air behind the one who must be their leader.

"Aviella," Rafe growls.

"Don't worry," I say, distracted by the flood of thoughts and images.

"About that," he says.

Nate hovers a dozen feet away, sword held ready but somehow, he senses the need to wait. The mages are pouring power into my shield reinforcing and expanding it. The leader of the birdmen and I stare at each other coming to an understanding.

We help, when can.

When I nod my understanding, he smiles.

You... the one. We... you...

There are no more words, what he conveys, there aren't words to contain. It's a rush, lifting me up magically and spiritually to another plane. Above and beyond, hero worship, admiration, love, they all pale and are inadequate to describe the sensation.

It's clear that they can't work against the Shadow directly, but they will help anywhere they can. They're an ally, but they're shackled by the very nature of their creation. They are Shadow-tainted, which is why they've stayed away. The Shadow could, potentially, control them. It could use them against me. That's why they've stayed clear, but in this case, they could help.

Bowing at my waist, I convey my appreciation. He smiles, which is still creepy as hell, ally or no, then the flock twirls and flies away. The butterflies dancing in my stomach leave me feeling a little sick. Rafe lowers his sword and turns to me as Nate lands next to us.

"What was that?" Nate asks.

"They're... birdmen," I say, lamely.

"Thanks, I totally missed that part," Rafe grins.

"Aviella, are they an enemy or not?" Nate asks, glaring at Rafe.

"No," I say. "Not really."

"Not really?" Nate asks.

"No," I say, shaking my head, still processing all that I've learned.

"We should go inside," Rafe says, yelling to be heard over the wind.

"Right," I agree. "I'm starving."

Rafe leads the way and I follow, digging through my thoughts as I figure out what is going to be next. This world is still full of surprises, for sure. Something about the birdmen and our words rings deeply true to me, and that's what I need to figure out.

They've forgiven. They've sacrificed. What am I going to have to sacrifice to save the world? What am I willing to?

CHAPTER TWENTY-FOUR

AVIELLA

"We have to go," Ronan says. "We'll be watching, the best we can."

"Thanks," I say, forcing a smile.

"The astral planes aren't safe," Killian says. "Avoid using them."

"Great," I say, shaking my head. "What is safe nowadays?"

"Not a lot," Gavin says.

He holds his arms out and I embrace him tightly. He kisses the top of my head then steps back. I embrace Killian and Ronan, bidding them each goodbye. It always sucks when people leave.

"How is Rowan?" I ask, the familiar ache in my chest the instant I think of her.

"She's great," Ronan says. "You won't believe it when you see her again. She's really growing in power."

"Good," I say, melancholy settling over me. "Keep her safe, okay? I don't know that you should bring her back around me."

"Aviella," Luca says, taking my hands in his. "It's going to work out."

"Right," I say, not willing to continue an argument about it.

The four of them exchange a look but no one says anything more. Which is fine with me. The three mages group together, and then with a simple poof they teleport away leaving Luca and me.

"What would you like to do?" he asks, still holding my hands.

His hands are warm but rough, covered in callouses. The simple connection calls up his memories, the ones I've shared with him. It's weird that I know things he has never said to me. Things I don't have a way to, but I do, like I know those callouses are from years of wielding a sword.

When I meet his eyes, the connection between us pulses, drawing us closer together. Our bodies never move, but in my head, we're kissing. The distance in his eyes makes it clear he's there with me. We're experiencing each other on another plane than this one.

"Food," I say, splitting my attention between the here and the there.

There, he's slowly undressing me, touching my body in all the right places. Here, we walk hand-in-hand to the dining car.

"I think we should celebrate," Rafe says as we enter the car.

Luca moves away but his fingers linger on my hand, reluctant to relinquish the contact. My hand feels cool and empty without his in it.

"Celebrate what?" I ask.

"Exactly," Rafe says, grinning broadly.

"You realize that's not an answer, right?" I ask, trying to focus and not let my body in the here react to what's happening in the there, with Luca.

"But it is, my dear," he says, pulling a large box out of a

cabinet. He throws the box open and begins to empty its contents onto the table. Suddenly he stops, looking at me with a piercing gaze and narrowing eyes then at Luca.

"What?" I ask, heat rising on my chest and cheeks.

"Would you two mind? If you're not bringing enough to share with the class, it's rude," he says.

Luca bursts out laughing while my cheeks turn fiery, and I can't meet Rafe's gaze. Weird to be embarrassed now of all times, but here I am, flushing cherry red.

"I'm sorry," Luca says.

"Oh, don't be," Rafe says. "If we'd rather that than dinner, I'm all in."

I have to change the subject before I literally burn from the embarrassment. Rafe's grin is lascivious and full of promises I know very well the demon can deliver on, but that's not what I want, not right now.

"Celebration," I say. "Let's celebrate. I want to bring all the survivors into it though."

"All of them?" Rafe asks, suddenly serious.

"Yes, all of them. This may be our last chance."

"Last chance?" Luca asks. "What do you mean, Aviella?"

I try to form words to describe this sensation.

"We're about to enter yet another bunker," I say, shrugging, struggling to figure out how to say it. "At every one before this, I've lost more and more. I've lost a lot of them on the journey too."

"Sure," Luca says, while Rafe only watches.

There's a deep understanding in Rafe's eyes that goes well beyond sympathy. He doesn't feel sorry for me, he gets it. He too feels this soul-deep sadness that I can't even begin to make Luca understand.

"Let's celebrate. Tonight, we'll be in the moment. The right now, only. Tomorrow will be what tomorrow is going to be," I say, unable to tear my eyes away from Rafe.

The understanding, the shared depth of our emotion binds us.

"A sound idea," Rafe agrees. "I'll get Efram to help me prepare the meal."

He walks away, leaving me with Luca. He has a half smile on his face that is enticing, but I'm not in the mood for more of that. The empty, aching sadness is consuming, and on some level, welcome. I need this, to remind myself of what it's going to take to do what must be done. I have to be willing to lose it all.

"Deep thoughts?" Luca asks, pulling out a chair and taking a seat next to me.

"Yeah," I say. "I guess so."

I sigh and do my best to pull myself out of it. We sit in an easy silence, and then Rafe returns with Efram and the four of us set about making a meal to celebrate... nothing really, but better to celebrate what we have than to focus on what we've lost.

"AND THAT'S THE STORY OF HOW THE PLATYPUS LAID EGGS AND was still a mammal," Rafe says with a flourish.

The crowd of people laughs. Their mood is the lightest it's been since leaving Tynan's bunker. On one hand they're probably numb from all the loss, but on the other we've given them some relief. A break from the looming fear.

On that note though, I wanted them here to talk to them. I get up on my feet and wait until all the gathered eyes turn to me and silence falls. I smile as I gather my thoughts, putting the pieces together and trying to figure out the best way to say what has to be said.

"Hey," I start out in a great style and aplomb. I'm sure all the great speeches of history started out with a 'hey'.

There are murmurs of greetings back to me, but they wait for me to say more.

"Look, we're about to enter New Jerusalem," I say. "I don't know what we're going to have to face. I'm sure there will be more trials. More difficulties. More reasons to give up.

"No matter what, all I can offer you, is that what you do matters. It may not matter in this world," I motion around us with one hand. "This place has gone to hell, literally. It may not matter here but there is more than this."

"Like what?" one of the men asks. "What is the point?"

"The point is that we can be better," I say. "You can be better. You have to—"

A loud scraping sound on the roof cuts me off. My magic is at my command, filling the room, causing the assembled survivors to gasp. I form magic around my fist, looking at the ceiling and waiting for any signs of a breach.

The scraping sound continues, and the train car sways and creaks as if there's some massive weight on top of it. As fast as it came, the sounds stop. The car stops its awkward motion. It sounds like footsteps walking down the roof. Then a figure drops past the window outside the rear door.

The door slides open as I raise my fist to unleash a magical bolt on whoever or whatever comes through. The magic releases as the shadowy figure steps inside, and I'm barely able to pull it back.

"Tynan!" I exclaim, as the dragon steps into the light.

He's dressed immaculately, not a hair out of place. His perfectly trimmed dark beard, kept short and barely past the five o'clock shadow, breaks with his smile. He straightens the cuffs of his shirt, pulling them past the sleeves of his jacket while looking over the scene before him.

"I see I'm in time for dinner," he says, striding to stand next to me at the head of the table.

I throw my arms around him and choke on all the words I

want to say. His wild, raging magic curls around me, intertwining with mine, caressing my skin with subtle warmth. He wraps his arms around me tightly, then pulls back far enough that he can claim my lips.

I don't care that everyone is watching. In his arms, none of it matters. He dominates my world, pushing out all those other concerns of appearances. If they don't like it, they can leave.

"Good to see you too," he says, breaking the kiss.

Gently he releases his tight grip, pulling me around to stand by his side while keeping an arm around my shoulders.

"Welcome back," Silas says.

"Didn't expect you yet," Rafe adds.

The survivors are preening and straining to have his attention while trying desperately not to appear to be trying at all. He takes them all in, his gaze lingering on each one in turn. As he reaches the last one his jaw tightens.

"Twenty-one?" he asks, his voice edging to a growl.

"It's been an interesting trip," Nate says.

"Fill me in later," he says. He pulls out a chair and waits for me to take it before pushing me in and taking his own seat at the head of the table. "Please, continue as you were."

He reaches out and takes a plate for himself and fills it with food. The survivors scramble to be the one to dish the items onto his plate for him. He watches them, and by his face I'd say it was amusement, but that's his mask. I'm in tune with him, connected, and I know he's angry and upset about the losses. A good leader or not, in his own way, he cared for those in his bunker.

"How long will you stay?" I ask.

"Not long," he says. "I had a brief moment and wanted to spend it here, with you." His eyes bore into mine for a long, intense moment before he looks around the table. "All of you."

I'd swear the survivors were going to break their necks they're gawking so hard. Still, it's nicer of him than he ever would have been before. He's changed. I suppose getting rid of a Shadow mark will do that for you.

I smile and we all eat with small talk resuming. No one brings up the bunker we're heading into and I don't see saying anymore either. I've said what I can. They're going to have to figure it out themselves. I only hope they make good choices.

Hell, I hope I make good choices. I'm as lost as the rest of them, even though everyone is looking to me to save the world.

The meal finishes shortly, and the survivors go to their bunks in the other car. Tynan rises to his feet, holding his hand out for me. I take it before I think about it. Only after my hand is in his do I feel the weight of the others' eyes on me. This is awkward.

"I would like some time with Aviella," he says, his voice resonating with something I can only call desire. "Are there any objections?"

My cheeks warm and my other hand clenches under the edge of the table, waiting for the responses that seem inevitable.

"Of course not," Silas says, ever the pragmatist.

"Alone? I'm happy to... help," Rafe grins.

"Efram and I have duties," Nate says, gripping Efram's shoulder.

Efram's face is clouded, but I can't read his thoughts even through our connection.

"I can help Nathanial," Luca says, as if he already knows what work needs to be done.

"Very good," Tynan says, pulling me along with him as he strides out of the train car.

He holds my hand tight, leading us away from the others. We pass through car after car.

"Where are we going?" I ask.

"You'll see," he says, without stopping.

We've gone through five different cars when he comes to a wall of crates. He motions with one hand, and the crates move aside, rearranging themselves to reveal an ornate locked door. He pulls a key out of his pocket, unlocks it, then steps to one side, motioning me inside.

"Oh," I gasp when I see what's on the other side of that lavish door.

I should have known. Tynan loves his luxuries, always indulges in them, and this is a testament to it. The entire room is done in crimson and dark wood. Teak maybe, or some other darker woods. The space is dominated by a massive four-poster bed replete with canopy that has gold tassels hanging off of it. The bed itself has a massively thick duvet and fluffy pillows all across it. It looks warm and inviting even from here.

"Do you like it?" Tynan asks, coming up behind me.

He's close. So close I can feel him, but he's not touching me, not yet. His energy presses against me, as I know his body will press against mine soon.

"It's beautiful," I say, turning into him.

"It doesn't compare," he says, and I flush fully for the first time. "It's been hell being separated from you."

"I've missed you, too," I say.

"Alaric and Shen send their regards," he says, his lips claiming mine.

As our bodies connect, suddenly I feel Shen and Alaric there with us, in spirit as much as body. As he slowly undresses me, the four of us are joining on the astral level, quadrupling the sensations. This new thing that started with Luca, this is something I could get used to…

CHAPTER TWENTY-FIVE

AVIELLA

I wake up covered in the unbelievable softness of the sheets and blankets of Tynan's bed. My head rests on his chest, and he has one arm wrapped around my shoulders. I snuggle closer to him, listen to his heartbeat, and let myself wake up slowly. There's no need to rush these things, at least not today.

"I'm glad you're here," I say.

"Me too," he says.

"Will you be able to stay," I ask, running my fingers through the hair on his chest.

"I'm afraid not," he says.

"Oh," I say, accepting the bad news.

We lie in silence, waiting for... something. I don't know what, actually, but I don't feel like facing the day. Not yet. I know we're close to the next bunker. This train ride has been stressful, but in a way, it's been a relief. A break from the pressures of every bunker I've been in. This one could be the worst of all of them though.

"Things are happening," Tynan says. "Faster than we expected. The Shadow is accelerating its plans."

"Are you surprised?" I ask.

"Yes," he says.

Silence falls again but now it's heavy with unspoken words. Finally, I force myself to sit up, pulling the blanket over my chest for warmth more than modesty.

"So, what's happening?" I ask, shifting to look at him.

He grimaces, moving his arms behind his head and stretching. It calls attention to the hard lines of his ripped body. A distraction I don't doubt he is doing on purpose, but I'm not going to be deterred.

"More bunkers have fallen," he says.

"How many?" I ask, sensing something unspoken.

"Most," he admits.

"Oh," I say, trying to not think of how many lives that would equate to.

How many innocent or mostly innocent people I failed to save. Cold seeps out of my core, slipping through my limbs like the embrace of a chilled lover. Familiar and not necessarily unwelcome.

"We're reaching a breaking point," Tynan says. "It will happen soon."

"What do you mean?" I ask.

"Soon, one side or the other will have such an advantage that they will sweep the board. Game over. None of the rest of it will matter."

"Which, right now, is the Shadow," I state, not ask.

"Yes," he agrees, pushing himself into a sitting position.

I can't help but notice the way the blankets pool across his legs, barely covering his manhood. It'd be nice to give myself over to baser desires and not worry about anything at all. It'd be nice but there is no time.

"How do we stop it?" I ask.

"We don't," he says. "You are the key. We are only supporters to the star of the show." He trails his fingers along my spine making me shudder. "Words I never thought I would say."

"Which ones," I ask.

"Admitting I'm not the star of the show," he smiles grimly. "Only you."

I start to say something but then realize I have nothing. What do you say in response to something like that? Warmth suffuses me as he embraces me in magic, and my own rises, responding to his.

"Thank you," I say at last.

"It's not a final end," he says. "Not yet, but the future has been blocked from me. I'm only seeing hazy possibilities."

"You can see the future? You never told me that," I say.

"I never told you a lot of things," he says. "But no, I no longer can see the future."

"What happened?" I ask.

"There is too much flux," he answers. "There is nothing that is set, every decision all of us make are changing it as fast as it settles."

"Oh," I say, thinking it over. "So we might win?"

"We might," he says.

"Or not."

"Or not," he agrees.

He climbs out of the bed, finds his pants and dresses. I follow suit, thinking over his words.

"I've had a…" I trail off unsure how to say what I want. "feeling? Sense?"

"Of?" he asks.

"Loss," I say. "Doom, maybe. Finality, I guess."

He nods and comes to take my hands in his.

"A crossroads is coming. The choices you make now will set the path of the world. I don't know what will be required of you, Aviella, but it won't be easy. I rest in the comfort of knowing you will do the right thing. No matter the cost."

The weight of it all settles onto my shoulders, and I bow my head.

"Thanks," I say, squeezing his hands.

Sighing, I square my shoulders and hold my head high. No matter the burdens laid down on me, I will bear them. That distant sense of doom is out there, but I'll face it when I have to.

CHAPTER TWENTY-SIX

AVIELLA

*R*afe and Tynan depart together. We don't make long goodbyes. That's something I don't think I could handle right now. A quick hug and kiss, and they leave. I know they'll be back, but what is coming up isn't for them to face. It's on me.

The land outside the window slowly gives way to something more alive. Spotty green-brown grass is the first sign of life, and it slowly takes over the blasted landscape. Massive spikes have been driven into the ground every fifty feet along the train track. Crude iron cages hang from the top of them, swaying in the wind. In the first ones rest aged skeletons.

As we travel further, more of the cages are filled with bodies that still have flesh on them. Murders of crows peck at the flesh, cawing and fighting over the choicest bits. My stomach roils at the grim sigils of what we're entering.

The land is rolling hills now and dusk settles across it. I'd guess we're getting close to the bunker. I have nothing else to do but wait and try to avoid looking out the window. I'd give anything for a distraction. The train lurches and comes to a stop. When I dare a glance outside, I immediately regret it.

A man's feet with a massive nail driven through them are the first thing I see, and bile rises in my throat. I want to look away, don't want to see more, but I can't tear my eyes away. It's a wreck that you can't stop yourself from witnessing.

When I bend over for a better look, more of the atrocity comes into view. It's every bit as bad as I feared it would be. The man is crucified, nailed to a cross, but the worst part is, he's alive. He hangs limply, his head on his chest, blood and tears streaming down his face. He's so gaunt I can count his ribs, but his chest continues to rise and fall.

A hand on my shoulder makes me jump, and my magic rises defensively.

"Woah," Luca exclaims, jumping back and holding his hands up before himself.

I force the magic back down, shake my head, fight back the tears. They keep welling up, the pressure swelling my throat. Luca understands. He steps forward and wraps his arms around me. He pulls me tight, and I lay my head on his chest until I get myself under control.

"Sorry," I say, when my throat relaxes.

"It's fine," he says, letting me go.

We move to the car where the passengers are gathered, waiting to disembark. Silas is standing by the exit, looking grim.

"Everyone listen," he orders. "We're about to enter New Jerusalem. This is much different than Tynan's bunker where you came from. You must be careful. No smile here is what it seems—it will not touch their eyes. Be very careful who you trust or connect to emotionally. It will be a test.

"If you practice any spirituality besides what they profess, hide it. Do not let them know. If you are branded a heathen, we will not be able to protect you.

"Be smart. We'll keep an eye on each of you as much as we can, but understand this—we are not in control here."

Murmurs of assent meet his words, but their fear is palpable, dark wings fluttering against me. Silas locks eyes with me. Understanding passes between us as I steel myself to face what is outside that door. As ready as I can be, I decide I'll take the lead. I need to set the tone for these survivors. Show them how to not be afraid but be obedient too.

Silas nods his approval, opening the door and stepping to one side. Butterflies war in my stomach, bile threatens to rise, but I ignore that and even the cold sweat dripping down my spine. Shoulders square, head high, I stride out to meet my fate.

There are three steps to the ground. I take them carefully, watching my surroundings both with my eyes and my magical sight. There's ambient magic around me that creates a pressure, as if something is forcing me to be smaller, less than I am. It pushes in, subtly, against my magic. It's frightening.

A massive rusty steel door is set into a grass-covered mound. It's big enough for two semis to pass through side by side. Burn marks, graffiti, and most disturbingly, deep gouges cover the doors. I stride towards them as Luca jumps off the train and moves to my side.

"Stop," a voice commands before I make two strides.

I comply, looking for the source.

Twelve red-robed men pop up almost magically. If not for my magical sight I might have considered it magic, but there was no surge, and I caught the last one appearing out of a secreted hole where they obviously can wait and watch new arrivals.

All twelve of them have large hoods that hide their faces in shadow, loose fitting so I can't tell their size or if they're armed under the robes. They each carry a lit, blood-red candle held in both hands clutched before them.

The survivors unload behind me huddling into a group. Our group stares at theirs, waiting, letting them have the first move and at least the appearance of control. My magic crawls across my skin, wanting to be unleashed, instinct screaming at me to not do this. Anything but submit to them. That instinct is enhanced by Tynan's magic which isn't making this easy.

The twelve begin a humming, chanting sound that's like a low rumble around us. No one moves as we wait. I'm not sure what's happening, but there's no magic building so I'm trying to remain calm. No easy task.

Luca shifts next to me, and then his magic softly mingles with mine like the gentlest of a lover's touches. It soothes the itching, crawling sensation pushing me to act. Let these weirdos have their ritual. First rule of dealing with fanatics, don't interrupt their rituals.

Okay, it's a new rule for me, but it seems like a good one. I'll note it down if I ever have a notebook for keeping weird rules in. At last the one in the more or less middle steps forward, stopping two paces in front of me. I force a smile that I hope is friendly.

"Hi," I say.

He raises his candle up to his hood where I still can't see his face, then blows out the flame. He slides the candle into the rope belt at his waist moving in a ritualistic manner. I clench my teeth, biting off my snarky comments. This is not the time Avi, don't be stupid.

He grabs both sides of his hood and then in a flourish throws it from his head, dropping his arms to his side. He's a middle-aged man with almost more gray than dark left in his hair. His face is tanned and covered with subtle scars that crisscross each other making strange patterns. He has cold, steel gray eyes that bore into me as if he has already judged and found me wanting.

"Welcome to New Jerusalem," he says with no warmth or hint of welcome in his voice.

"Thank you," I say.

"We are the devout followers of He Who Has Risen," he continues. "Only the faithful may pass through our gates. Unbelievers will be handled with the righteous fury of the One."

My stomach clenches tight as the breeze decides to bring to me the scent of death and decay that surrounds us. It's a terrible accent to his words, making it clear how they deal with unbelievers. Behind me the fear of the survivors is thick. I don't blame them. I'm almost afraid too. Almost.

"I understand," I say, unsure of my part to play in this ritual.

He grimaces, his eyes moving up and down my body, and if the situation was any different, I'd say he was checking me out to see if I'd be a good lay, but there's not a hint of the erotic in his gaze. I'm left again with that sense of having been found wanting in his eyes. I quickly push down the urge to strike him down with my own righteous fury.

Innocents. There are Innocents here and we need to find them, plus this is the next clue to finding my dad. I'll do what I must.

"All must be judged," he says. "Leave all weapons you may have outside. Inside the haven of New Jerusalem you will not need them. If any of you are witches, declare yourself now, so you may be properly judged."

Witches? What in the holy fuck is that supposed to mean?

"Witches?" I ask, tilting my head to one side.

"Those who deal with the arts arcane," he says. "Like you."

Those last two words fall heavy almost hitting me with force. I swallow hard and stand a little straighter.

"Right," I say.

He scans the assembled crowd, but no one seems to stand

out to him, not even Luca, Silas, or Efram. Why did he single me out?

"Come inside," he says, "you are welcome to partake in the grace of He Who Has Risen. His love and care will embrace you as long as you find your true faith, which will be in him. You will be educated, you will learn his words of wisdom. This is your chance for true salvation."

Every word makes my skin crawl. I'm all for faith, for sure, belief in a greater good. Some force no matter what you call it, but this is different. There's a hollowness to his words, an unthinkingness that actually scares the hell out of me.

The twelve robed men form a double line and we're motioned to walk down it towards the doors of the bunker. I'm so busy looking around I stumble over a rock and bump into one of the men forming the line. I hit something hard and metal that clanks.

A gun.

A big gun. Great. That makes the warm welcome even more ominous. Straightening I take deep, calming breath and exchange a glance with Luca. His eyes narrow, crinkling his nose, as I glance at the mid-section of the man I bumped. His robe shifted when I hit him, and I can see the outline of what looks like an assault rifle under it now.

Luca smiles broadly and we continue walking. The doors open with a loud screech of resistance taking two men to pull on it before it does. The man with his hood down leads us into the dark tunnel. I wish it didn't look like we were walking into the mouth of doom.

We pass through and gather into an open area. It's not much different from every other bunker I've been in except everyone in sight is wearing white robes. They all have this serene smile on their faces too. Only the man in red looks grim. He turns to face us.

"Before you can be accepted," he says, his voice echoing

off the steel walls around us. "You must be tested. We will not accept the unclean."

"What does that mean?" I ask, stepping forward.

He frowns deeply and shakes his head, sighing as if I'm the greatest burden he's ever been asked to bear.

"You will be tested," he says, motioning to one side. "Form a line there."

We line up as ordered. I'm not going to get answers from him, and at this point the only option is to comply. Comply or go back outside, and it's not like things are rosy out there either. Two of the red robes approach and take my arms. I let them lead me away, though every part of me wants to jerk away from their hands. They feel slimy, gross, and disgusting.

They take me down a hall that is dimly lit. More of the white robes, with that passive fixed smile walk by us, nodding as they see us. It's quieter here as we walk, and somehow it doesn't seem so bad. I'll be okay here, I'm sure. This is a good place after all.

We stop at a door on the left and one of them knocks. A moment later, on some hidden signal, they open the door and sandwich me between them as we enter. It's an office setting with a nice desk that has two chairs in front of it. The walls are a soft creamy color that is very soothing.

One of the red robes motions to a chair which I take gratefully. Behind the desk is an empty chair and the two red robes leave the room, closing the door. It's fine, gives me time to look around. There is a low bookcase behind the desk that has a few pieces of art on it, a vase of fake flowers, and above it is a framed print of a man.

This man is impressive. There's something about him that feels right. He's looking back at me with a serious, thoughtful expression. Almost there seems to be a halo around his head. The planes of his face are soft, but his eyes are deep and soulful. A half smile is on his lips as if he knows something I don't. I'm sure he does.

A portion of the wall to my right opens behind the desk and an elderly man walks in. He must be in his eighties. He's bent with age, his face is wrinkled and worn. He shuffles in then takes a seat behind the desk. He picks up a clipboard and appears to be reading it with great interest.

"So," he says, at last. "Welcome to New Jerusalem, founded by He Who Has Risen."

"Thank you," I say, feeling very complacent. He continues staring at the clipboard.

"It appears, you are in need of…. Cleansing."

He pauses before he says the word but the way he says it makes me tilt my head in confusion and concern.

"Cleansing?" I ask.

"Yes, I'm afraid so," he says, looking up and squinting at me. "You're very… unclean."

Pressure builds in my head and some part of me wants to explode. Tear this place down for daring to try to judge me. Don't they know I'm… no, that's the Dragon magic. That's not me. I'm feeling thick. It's hard to think through an entire thought.

"That sounds bad," I say.

"Oh," the old man says. "It is what it is. None are turned away by He Who Has Risen but the uncleaned must be washed in blood so that they may emerge into his Holy Light."

I'm struggling to clear my head, but I can't figure out what's happening. I'm tired, really really tired, and would like to lie down somewhere. Take a nice long nap.

"I'll do what I must," I say, remembering that I'm here for a purpose.

I'm supposed to integrate to this place. Become part of it so I can find the Innocents. If there are any, or maybe there are a lot? Like, all these people are innocent, aren't they? I mean, look how holy they are. The emptiness in my stomach aches, but I'm too tired to care.

"Good," the old man says, laying down the clipboard. "That's very good."

He smiles and his eyes look like empty black pits with pupils that are entirely too large. There's no warmth to his smile, but that's okay, I'll be fine.

"I'm assigning you to Purgatory. Work hard and you'll earn your way out of there in no time."

"Purgatory?"

Deep behind all my other thoughts, something screams that this is wrong. I should be upset but I'm not.

"Yes, dear," he says. "You'll need to be cleansed so you can fully join us. We'll take care of you, if you don't betray the blood."

"What would that mean?" I ask, confused.

"You'll attend daily lessons, that will all come clear," he says.

"What about my friends?" I ask.

"I don't know," he says. "Once they've been tested, they'll be assigned an appropriate floor for them to work and study on.'

"I see," I say.

"Good," he says. "Now let's get you settled."

He motions a hand, and two men in red robes with their faces hidden enter the room. They take me by each of my arms and lead me away. Somehow, it doesn't seem as bad this time as it did the last time.

CHAPTER TWENTY-SEVEN

AVIELLA

*D*ays seem to fly past. It's hard to keep track of them. It's hard to remember that I'm supposed to be doing something. I'm so busy with my work and my studies. There's no time for anything else, really. It's been three, no four days since I saw the guys.

It's fine though. This work is hard, but man it really needs to be done. I pause to wipe the sweat from my brow before I resume scrubbing the machine part in my hands. I could do this so much faster with my magic.

As fast as I think it, the part floats out of my hand and magic energy scrubs over it. The lights of the room flash blinking red, and an alarm sounds. Oh, no!

"Oh, I'm sorry!" I cry out before they reach me.

Sorry doesn't cut it. I know better than to do that. It's against the word of He Who Has Risen. The backlash hits before I can brace for it. Every muscle tenses as the volts of electricity race through my body. Pain, pure, cleansing pain is all that I know.

When at last it passes, the others leaning away from me to

avoid my punishment sit back up and resume their duties. Tears streaming down my face, I go back to work too.

～

"AND THEN HE ROSE, RISING ABOVE THE DEMONS AND THE unclean, he stood above them all in his shining glory," Brother Timmon continues the sermon, reading from the Holy Book.

The pressure in my head is constant but I'm used to it now. It's so hard to concentrate. I need to learn every word of this book. I must be able to quote passages by heart. I have to show He Who Has Risen that I am cleansed.

Aviella...

A voice whispers in my head, but that only tells me I'm not cleansed yet. The unclean still has its deep, taloned claws inside of me. I'm not worthy yet. I will be.

Something stirs deep inside pushing back against the pressure, but Brother Timmons feet appear in front of my bowed form.

"Aviella," he says. "Are you clean?"

"No, Brother," I sob. "I am not."

"No, you are not," he says. "Do you want to be?"

"Yes!" it tears out of me. "Oh, help me brother, yes!"

The pressure in my head is so great, I'm afraid it's going to explode. It would almost be a relief. Let it be over with. I'm not worthy as it is.

"I will," he says, laying a hand on the back of my head.

"Be cleansed!" he says, his hand tightening in my hair and pulling on it painfully dragging my head up with him.

Tears stream down my face, but that evil buzzing builds in my core. I try to fight it, but I can't control it. I'm trying, but then Tynan is in my thoughts, standing before me, and I'm with him, no longer here.

"You're falling for it," he says, his dark eyes drinking me in and filling my body with desire.

"Falling for it?" I ask.

Brother Timmons chants, jerking my head back and forth, chunks of my hair ripping out as he does.

"Their game," Tynan says. *"You're better than this, Aviella. Stronger. Fight, let your inner dragon roar."*

"I can't," I say.

I'm in two places at once. Here is pain, agony, and the pressure that won't stop. There I'm with Tynan, safe, protected, and so much more comfortable. It's tempting to stay there. To abandon here completely.

"If you do that," Tynan says, reading my thoughts. *"It's over. Lean on me girl, draw on my power."*

Dark, reddish wings spread from his back, appearing out of nowhere as he closes and pulls me into an embrace. His power races through me with a jolt.

The pressure is gone. My thoughts are clear. Timmons has left me to move on to another of the unclean. I'm shaking as power courses through, truly cleansing me. The pressure tries to push into my thoughts again, but this time I'm ready. As it tries to clamp down, understanding hits me.

It's magic. These sons of bitches! It's magic mind control. Pushing in, making me docile. I've bought into their game, but I'm done with that.

"Don't give it away, Avi. Be calm girl," Tynan's voice comes through my mind.

He's right. I need to control this burning rage. This desire to burn the entire bunker down myself. There are Innocents here. If they can push into my thoughts like this, then that means they can definitely hide the Innocents from the mages. I grit my teeth and lash a tight rein on my emotions.

"You are all dismissed to your quarters," Brother Timmons says. "Do not forget your ablutions."

"Yes, Brother," I intone with the rest.

Carefully, I rise, keeping my shoulders slumped and head down. I can't give away that I've broken their control. As a group, we shuffle out of the Chapel towards our rooms. Only when I've shut the door and taken my position kneeling next to my bed do I drop the act.

Rage leaves me shaking. I tell myself to let it go, and that it will do me no good to lose control. I know how bad it would be, and finally I let it run its course. It leaves behind a pulsing angry ember only waiting for the right breeze to burst into raging flames again.

Resting my head against the cool steel rail that forms the frame of my assigned twin bed with its rock-hard mattress, I try to come up with a plan. It's hard to think, still. The pressure is incredible. I don't know where the others are, it would be so much easier if I had them with me.

I reach out with magic to seek them, but I can't find them. After I clear my head, I focus on the flow of magic through my body, letting it course through my veins, and then try again. My awareness pushes out, elevating, changing as I reach towards the astral, for lack of a better term.

Obey. You are unclean. Only he can cleanse you of your sins. Confess.

It isn't words, really. It's entire thoughts being pushed in, pressing into me, appearing as if they're my own. Only with Tynan's power pulsing through my aura do I see the thoughts for what they are, not mine. This is the most frightening thing I've ever experienced.

All the death, the destruction, the danger... none of it compares to this. This invasion not only of my thoughts, but my very soul. Twisting who I think I am. All those around me are affected. I wonder if the pressure is as high on the other levels of the bunker, or if it's reserved for this special hell they've thrown me into.

I can't push past it, can't figure a way around, or a way out. I'm exhausted. Every part of me hurts. The hard, constant labor combined with the "Brothers" who torture us at the slightest sign of slipping. My eyes drift closed, and I awake with a start. I don't know how long I was out, but I'm getting nowhere doing this. When I stand, my lower back screams in pain. I try to stretch it out, but that only aggravates my thighs and butt.

I give up and lie down on the bed, curl into a ball, and cry myself to sleep.

CHAPTER TWENTY-EIGHT

LUCA

This is going to hurt.

It doesn't matter though, I'm going to go through it. Moving along with the crowd of people dressed in immaculate white, I wait for the right moment. As we filter through the doors to the dining hall, it seems as good a time as any.

I'm at least four floors over Aviella. It took me the last five days to figure out where they sent her, and the moment I did, my blood chilled. I didn't know to warn her to hide her nature better. She's not skilled in deception. If anything, she's the direct opposite of discreet, especially on the magical front. She's a golden beacon calling in the night, no matter how hard we've tried to obscure the signals pulsing out of her. Each time she's joined with one of her fated mates, her power has escalated exponentially, and the work of hiding her has become harder.

Now she could be a raging sun to anyone with magical sensitivity. The psychic pressure here is intense. I hope she was prepared. I have to count on Silas for that. I haven't seen him since our arrival either. The only other one of our group I've seen is Efram and occasionally Nathanial.

Efram is keeping his head down, watching and learning, but appears to be getting in well. Something about him seems off, but I can't put my finger on what. I haven't seen him in two days, but he was working directly with the leaders of this level of the bunker. Nathanial was immediately crowned as a Chosen one and swept to the upper floors, so I've only seen him once.

Well, here goes nothing. Grinning, I form a symbol in my mind to focus my magic, then let it rip. Flames explode around my body, outlining me as I run and leap onto one of the long cafeteria-style tables. I run down the length of it kicking off the trays of food as I go, screaming and waving my arms around like a damn fool.

The red guards react fast, but not fast enough. I leap and cavort around until they're close enough. I won't hurt anyone but them. Once they are...

I drop to a crouch, spinning on my knee, and thrust two hands at them with closed fists, directing a hard ball of magic into the mid-section of the closest. He flies backwards and slams against the far wall. The second guard hesitates, which is bad for him. I slam my fist up as if doing an uppercut even though he's still ten feet away. He reacts as if hit by a heavy-weight champion, flipping up and over, landing hard on his back.

The crowds of sheep scream, dropping to their knees and offering up prayers to He Who Has Risen. It's sad and pathetic and honestly makes my heart ache. They've been fooled and aren't strong enough of will to resist the magi-enforced will.

More guards appear, coming at me from all sides. I fight them for a while, holding back my true power. I'm not trying to win, after all, but I do want to make sure I've done enough damage to be labeled 'unclean' and sent to the lower floors.

Once I've done enough damage to feel certain of my fate, I stop and drop to my knees. Here comes the pain...

"THERE!" ONE OF THE HOODED RED GUARDS YELLS AS HE throws me through the door.

He steps in close enough to kick me in the ribs, breaking another one. I cough up blood and roll over with the force of it. Damn, this is painful.

"What have we here?" another voice asks.

Stars dance across my eyes, and every breath forces me to decide if I want to take it, knowing how much pain there will be the moment I do. There's a gurgling sound to accompany my own rasping as my lungs fill with blood.

"Another for your attention," says the same hooded guard who threw me. He spits on me. "He's unclean. Insane."

"Oh," the new voice says, kneeling and coming into my blurry vision. "This is most unfortunate. We'll fix you, won't we?"

He grips my jaw and forces me to look at him directly. I'm not in a condition to answer, so I don't, but he tightens his grip on my jaw until it's painful too.

"Won't we?" he asks, a malicious grin crossing his face.

"Yes..." I gasp, blood flecking his hand from my breath.

"Yes, what?" he asks.

Damn it, can't you all be done with your play so I can heal myself? This really hurts.

"Yes... sir," I say. I have to force the words out.

My wavering vision explodes, turning black with burgeoning stars, and my face burns. He slapped me, the son-of-a-bitch. Once we're done here, I'm going to reserve something special for this one.

"I am not a sir," he says. "You will call me Brother Timmons."

I don't answer him because I'm barely clinging to consciousness as it is. He seems to accept my silence as assent, though, because no more pain comes. I hate to admit I'm grateful, but damn it, I am.

"Take him to the infirmary," Brother Timmons says. "Tend his wounds. I want him on the line by the morning."

Rough hands grab hold and I'm carried away. Dimly I hear Brother Timmons talking to the guards who delivered me.

"He wants another sacrifice," one voice says.

"I've got a couple in mind," Brother Timmons says. "When?"

"Two, maybe three days," the other voice says.

"Plenty of time for me to make my choice," Brother Timmons says.

We move through a door, and the men carrying me bang my head against the doorframe. I lose track of the conversation, blacking out for a moment. I'm left with a sense of dread. Magic tingles its way through my body, slowly healing me. I can't let it go too fast or they'll notice.

They drop me on a hard bed, then turn and leave. Alone in the cold silence, I let the blackness take hold while my body works to put itself back together.

CHAPTER TWENTY-NINE

AVIELLA

*A*nother day. I'm on the line, as usual, but my, it's getting easier to think. I've constructed a kind of mental wall made of magical energy that holds the constant pressure at bay. It's helping, but the pressure and insidious thoughts continue to test the defense. It's draining, so I try not to think too much about it.

I've tried reaching out for the guys, but nothing. I can't even reach Tynan again. To say this sucks is an understatement. I haven't felt so lost and alone in a long time. It brings back memories of waiting in that shitty room for my Dad to come back.

It doesn't help that I have to watch myself every second not to let magic slip out. All my life I've had power, but I never understood it, and only recently have I had control of it. In that time though, I've gotten used to relying on it in ways I didn't notice. Little things, really. Magic greases the wheels of life and living.

No longer. The instant I slip, there will be pain. If I go under the lash again, it will be doubly hard to keep my wall up, and then I risk falling under their control again. One of the unclean in front of me trips and falls to her knees. I stop to help her up.

"Stop!" a deep voice orders.

The girl is crying, tears streaming down her face. When I touch her magic sparks between us. She's not powerful, but she does have it. She looks up, her eyes filled with despair. She's trembling. I pull, trying to help her back to her feet, but she's not helping.

Suddenly her eyes widen, her mouth drops open, and then my world explodes.

I hit the ground hard, jerking uncontrollably as the electricity courses through my nerves. Almost I black out, and part of me wishes I had. Anything to escape this hell I'm trapped in. Damn it, why did we even come here!

At last it stops. The pressure is there, so close, pushing, prodding, looking for an opening through my defenses. Panting, eyes clenched tight, I fortify my walls.

"Get up, plebe!"

Tears are running down my own face as I roll over onto my knees and slowly, painfully, force my way to my feet. One hand on the wall, I pant to catch my breath, but the line is moving and there's no time. Something warm passes over my skin and the pain recedes.

Straightening, I look quickly around and see Luca. He looks like total shit. His face is gaunt, yet swollen at the same time. One eye is completely shut. The other locks onto me and he smiles—or a bad imitation of a smile forms on his face.

One of the red-robed, hooded guards slams a fist into my shoulder twisting me back around. I shuffle along with the line going to my place at the workstation. Luca is only three people away. He's so close my heart leaps at seeing him, but an ache forms in my guts at the same time.

If he's in here, who's going to save me?

Another wave of magic lightly touches me, and I shiver involuntarily. It's cooling, soothing and so, so welcome. Maybe we can break out together? The others must be close. Maybe he came in to find me? A whisper passes down the line, but I'm too lost in my thoughts to catch what they're saying until a loud screech happens, jerking my attention.

"Unclean," Brother Timmons voice booms loud enough to be heard in the large work room.

"Yes Brother, we are unclean, unworthy of his saving grace," I intone with the others.

"A glorious moment will come soon," he says. "He Who Has Risen has made a request. A request for one of you to be cleansed by his holy blood. He will wash you of your sins and send you to your final fate cleansed and ready for judgement!"

"We are not worthy," the crowd says but my tongue is numb, and I can't get my mouth to work.

What is this? These people are all crazy but that sounds horrible. Terrifying even.

"I do not know which of you will be chosen, yet," Brother Timmons says. "But prepare yourselves. Be extra diligent in your ablutions, work extra hard so that you may be the Chosen One!"

"Yes Brother Timmons," the voices of the crowd sound as one.

I glance down the line and catch Luca's eye. This is bad. I can feel it in my bones, but I don't know what it means or what to do about it.

CHAPTER THIRTY

SILAS

"$\mathcal{H}$istorian," Tomas says, as he walks into my office. I look up from the scroll I'm reading, narrowing my eyes at the man. "Yes?"

"Uhm, s-s-sorry," he stutters. I don't respond, staring and letting him sweat. "Your presence is, uh, order--, uh, requested."

"I see," I say, carefully rolling the scroll.

Rising to my feet I walk over to the cabinet and lock the scroll safely back into place. It's not a valuable piece, really, but they seem to think it is, so I'll play the game and let them believe it. When I turn around Tomas stares at me with his hands clenched in front of himself, waiting. I also wait, willing to wait much longer than he is, I'm sure.

Suddenly he startles as if only then realizing we've been gazing at each other for the better part of a minute. He flushes a bright red edging on purple brought on by his poor circulation and impending diabetes. He turns around in a hurry, throws the door open, and leads the way out.

I follow him at a leisurely pace. He rushes ahead before realizing I'm not keeping up when he looks over his shoulder. He then rushes back to three paces in front of me. He tries to keep the pace I set after that. We make our way through the halls of the bunker. I've been afforded a place of some regard, but my inquiries after Aviella have been rebuffed. The only thing I've learned for sure is that she is among the unclean.

That doesn't sound good, but for now I have to put my trust in the training I've given her and her own resourcefulness. If something seriously happened to her, I'd know it, I'm sure. She's not one for subtlety in most cases.

We pass by one of the security rooms right as Nathanial walks out. I stop, waiting for him to close the door. He does and stares.

She is on the lowest levels. Nathanial passes to me mentally.

Is she okay? I ask.

Not for long.

I resume walking, but at the same time that Tomas realizes again that I'm not with him. My stomach churns bile as I play out possibilities. The path we're treading is treacherous. They've separated us, tossed Aviella to the lowest floors, and there is power here.

The power is the most surprising. I didn't expect such a force to be behind it. It's constant here, but from what I have ascertained on the lower levels it's even more intense. I only hope Aviella is okay. Tomas stops before a door and turns to face me. He's pale, sweat beading across his face.

"What is it?" I ask, eyes narrowing.

"He Who Has Risen," Tomas says, awe and reverence in his voice.

"Yes?" I ask.

"He awaits you, Historian," Tomas says. "Personally."

He's all but groveling before me, but my blood chills at his words. I didn't expect to come to the cult leader's attention, not this fast. This could play out good or bad. Steeling myself for the confrontation, I nod sharply to Tomas and enter the door without further waiting.

The instant I step through the door, I'm awash in mystical forces. It's whispering, insinuating, seeking cracks in my protections. I should worship this man. He is holy. He is the light.

He is a crackpot with power. All the rest is bunk spread by the man himself. I've seen his likeness, as it's literally everywhere through the bunker, though few ever see him in person. Seeing him, I know why. Whatever he's gone through has changed him dramatically, and not for the better.

The likenesses that are spread throughout the bunker are of a middle-aged man with gray at his temples, bright blue eyes, a lined face that portrays wisdom and deep thought. All the images are smiling, some more than others. They push the narrative of him being a chosen one.

In reality, the man before me is no longer good looking. He's barely human any longer. His once-blue eyes are a rich, piercing green that's on the edge of glowing with their own light. The skin of his face is pulled so tight I can make out indentations in his skull, giving him a skeletal appearance. He's gaunt as well but he projects a glamor that looks more like his expected images, which I see through easily.

I pretend I don't. I school my face to an appropriate appearance of awe at his supposedly holy presence and kneel before him as expected. Two guards stand behind him, doing their best to blend into the décor. He's powerful and obviously the source of the magic shielding the bunker.

"No, no, Historian," he says, placing a hand on my shoulder. "Rise now. You're not one to bow before my humble self. It is I who should bow to you, for what is closer to Heaven than knowledge?"

"I would not presume to know," I say, serious.

"Well, I do know," he assures me. "I was there, after all, but the Divine in His infinite grace and wisdom, sent me back here to shepherd the fallen."

"We're grateful," I say through gritted teeth.

He smiles, a brilliant grin in the glamor but behind it, his teeth are rotting. His face stretches with it, showing off scars. When I study him closer, there are scars peeking out from under his shirt. I file the knowledge away. There's something about them that tickles at my memory.

"Of course you are, now," he nods solemnly. "Be all that as it may, the Lord did not give me all knowledge. This is why I need men like you!"

"I am honored to serve," I say, playing my part while watching every move, studying.

"As you should be," he says. "But tell me, Historian, what do you know of the Shadow? Do you know some secrets that might help me?"

"That is a broad subject," I say, surprised by his question.

"So it is," he agrees, grimacing. "How about twelve?"

"Twelve what?" I ask.

"The Power of Twelve," he says. "Have you heard of such a thing?"

"No," I lie.

He grimaces and his eyes narrow like he realized I'm not being truthful. He moves close, too close, the stench of him is enough to make me gag, but I suppress the desire. He smells of chemicals, formaldehyde with hints of something else.

"Now Historian," he says, so close he's almost whispering in my ear. "Tell me what you know."

My skin crawls, he's so close. It's disgusting and disturbing.

"Well there is a historical significance to the number," I observe, filtering what is safe to tell him. "In Ancient Mesopotamia, the number was symbolic of the Gods. In many ancient cultures the number appears in relation to the spiritual and the arcane. In Astrology for instance."

"Yes, Historian, but why? That is the question you see. Why this number? What does it symbolize?"

He marches circles around the room, waving his hands in the air vaguely. The magical enforcement of his personality beats against my defenses. Quietly I reinforce them.

"It could symbolize many things," I say, deliberately vague.

"Of course it could," he says, whirling on a heel to face me. "But it's power, isn't it? One who wields twelve. That's what she said, that's what I need to know, and I need to know now."

"She said?" I ask, latching on to the one anomaly in his speech.

He frowns, shaking his head. "Nothing."

"If I knew more, I could be of more assistance, I'm sure. What are you looking for?"

Pull the strings. Something is very wrong. As subtly as I can, I reach out with my awareness. I'm testing the air around us but trying to avoid him noticing what I'm doing.

"The forces working against us!" he yells, throwing his arms in the air. "We know, they would betray us, they come for us, but we must be strong. We must be ready!"

He's yelling, all but frothing at the mouth. As my awareness reaches out, I recoil. Shadow, powerful Shadow, it was here and not long ago.

This is bad, worse than I expected. That's way too much concentrated power that stood in this room to leave that much of an impression on the ambient magic. My stomach drops to the floor and cold numbness deadens my limbs.

"Let me help," I offer.

"How do we know we can trust you?" he asks, his eyes

narrowing with suspicion. "You could be a spy like all the rest. Tell me what you know?"

He focuses and his power crashes against me. I stumble backwards, unprepared for the sudden onslaught. Reacting quickly I drop to my knees and take on the appearance of being subservient.

"What is it you need?" I ask, gritting my teeth as the onslaught continues.

"Where is she?" he asks. "Which one? Tell me, find her for me so I don't have to go to extremes. It'd be a shame, but I have to have the power for myself."

"Which power?" I ask.

"The power of twelve!" he yells, standing over me now, pouring his power down onto me with crushing force.

I restrain myself from lashing out. I've bowed before, many times through the years, sometimes it's the better part of valor. All I can think of is Aviella. I'm doing this for her. She's worth any price, including my pride.

"Of course," I say.

"It's a girl, I'm sure of that," he says, pacing away while musing. "I gleaned that much from the she-bitch but that's still a broad swath of possibilities."

He's talking about Aviella, of that I have no doubt, but who is the 'she-bitch'?

"What else do you know?" I ask, rising to my feet. "I want to help. Please, in the name of your Holy Light, tell me so I can."

He glances over his shoulder with narrowed eyes. He frowns deeply, then nods.

"The she-bitch wants her, that means power. She never wants anything but power. She only takes interest in things that will aid her conquest, but if I have it, then I can stand against her." He closes the space with me and grips my shoulders tight, his piercing eyes inches from my own. "I have to, you see, I'm the Chosen One. It all became clear when I rose again. I knew, right then, that I was on a path set by the Divine."

"And we are not worthy," I intone.

"No, you're not," he says. "None of the others survived. I alone rose, I was the one returned. I can't do it alone though, I need the flock of the cleansed. I need the power of twelve to fulfill my destiny. Nothing is set in stone. It can change, it must change!"

"I will help," I say.

"Good," he nods enthusiastically. "Good."

He lets me go, turning away. He strides to his desk keeping his back to me.

"Go, find her," he says. "Hurry."

I don't wait for further instructions before I race out of the room.

CHAPTER THIRTY-ONE

NATHANIAL

"Can you look through past footage?" Silas asks.

He's pale, shaken, something I never would have thought possible.

"It is difficult," I say. "But not impossible."

"Good, I need you to go back through the last twelve hours. Someone visited this bunker."

"That is not as unusual as you would think," I say. "What has happened?"

"Aviella is in danger," he says, grimly. "He Who Has Risen is looking for her, specifically. Someone or some thing turned him onto her presence here. Someone knows she is here, and they want her."

"How do you know this?" I ask.

"He called me in for an interview," he says.

"Personally?" I ask.

"Yes," he nods.

My heart beats faster. "I will do what I can."

Silas nods sharply then fades out of the astral.

"Nate, what are you doing, daydreaming? We got work to do here!" Walter says.

"Yes," I agree. "Of course."

I lean forward and stare at the monitors attentively. Walter settles back into his chair staring at his bank. Gently I caress his thoughts with a breath of the Divine, clouding his attention. A smile forms on his face as he goes to a happy place in his head.

Glancing over and satisfying myself that he is fully occupied, I turn to finding the information that Silas is asking for, but first I check the monitors for the lower levels.

Aviella shuffles along with a line, head down, shoulders hunched. Her hair hangs loose, dirty and ratted. My heart aches looking at her, but she's alive. Right now that's the best I can do for her. Luca walks three people behind her. He looks up and right into the camera. His face is swollen almost the point of being unrecognizable. He nods sharply, letting me know he senses my watching.

Satisfied with nothing more I can do to help, I call up the cameras on the entrance halls and play back the footage. Walter stirs, and I give him a fresh breath of Divine while I continue my search for the newcomer. Several people come and go through the entrance, but then there's a blip that stops my attention on it.

The blip keeps happening. I play it back over and over. The time counter in the corner jumps almost a minute. Something is off. I watch that tiny segment again and again, but each viewing the same thing happens. I call on the Divine and wrap myself in a protective shield, then watch it again.

This time it plays through. My heart stops.

Her.

She was here, herself.

She's beautiful, every bit as beautiful as I remember her when I last saw her, eons ago, calling for us all to join her rebellion. She smiles at the greeters, striding in, arrogant as if this is her own home. Her head held high, shoulders squared, her chest thrust out. She doesn't even bother bringing body-guards. What guards could she bring that would compare to her own power?

She walks through the halls and I follow her, going from camera to camera. I have to refresh the patterns shielding me several times to be able to follow her. At last she walks into the office of He Who Has Risen where there are no cameras.

I watch the seconds tick by with bated breath. She's in there for exactly one minute, six seconds, six tenths of a second. The symbolism isn't lost on me but only adds to the chills racing through my body. She stops in the antechamber and stares into the camera.

I was cold before, but now I'm frozen. Paralyzed as she stares directly at me and the memories flood back. She was so powerful, so beautiful, then she rebelled. I wanted to follow her. Wanted to, but I didn't. She was wrong, her arrogance so great it blinded her.

This is bad. This is as bad as it gets. We're racing for the end, and this makes it clear that no more punches are being pulled. Why didn't she grab Aviella while she was here?

Something must be holding her back....

Free will. Of course. The one thing she will not break. She has to be given Aviella by someone with free will, other-wise she would be breaking her own rules.

I reach out to Silas on the astral. He needs to know she was here. In person.

CHAPTER THIRTY-TWO

AVIELLA

*A*ll I want to do is find my Dad. That doesn't seem so hard, right? I know, deep in my soul, that he's out there. He's alive and finding him shouldn't be that big of a deal. Except the entire world seems dead set on keeping me from getting there.

Twenty-four hours of whispers about who will be chosen. What it means to be chosen. Most, if not all, seem to be looking forward to it. I can't blame them. The constant pain, the mental assault to comply, the monotony of the days is numbing. Death would be a release at least.

Having seen the 'unclean' outside this place, I have no doubt that's where it will end. It won't be fun or nice or relaxing. It will be a hard, painful death, but I can't deny that even to me there's an appeal. I've only been here for days, a week maybe. Some of these people have been here for god knows how long. My heart aches every time I look at them. I try not to, in all honesty, because I can't stand the pain they bring with them.

Lying on the rock-hard mattress and staring at the back of my eyelids, I reach out for any of the guys. I cast myself quietly into a happier place and hope that one of the guys will make it to me. I call to them, willing any of them to please, please join me. Give me that much of a break from the living hell I'm in.

As the astral forms around me, taking on the aspect of a cozy bedroom replete with a big screen television and a comfy chair to curl up in to read, Efram appears.

"Efram!" I cry out.

"Avi! Thank god!" he races to me, wrapping his arms around me and crushing me against him.

I can't hold back my tears of relief and joy seeing him. When I hold him, his scent is pure joy. The feel of his arms around me create a small moment of safety and relief. We cling to each other with a desperation borne of despair. I don't want to let him go, and for his part he doesn't release me.

I don't know how long we stand, holding tight, but at last he eases his grip. Reluctantly I step out of his arms but keep my fingers on his biceps. That simple touch making him real, I need it. So damn badly, I hate to admit it.

"Are you okay?" I ask.

He snorts, shakes his head. "You're asking me? How are you? How bad is it?"

I look away, unable to meet his eyes. I can't lie to him, but I don't want to think about it either.

"Luca has been hurt pretty bad," I say, side-stepping the actual question he asked, glancing at his face quickly to see if he'll buy into it.

He frowns, and it's clear he doesn't miss what I'm doing, but then he nods.

"How bad?" he asks, granting me the no-answer.

"His face is a mess," I say. "He'll survive. I don't doubt he's been through worse, but still it looks bad."

"Right," Efram says.

It's easier to focus on someone else. My own problems become less when I'm worried about one of my guys, or anyone else really.

"Do we have a plan yet?" I ask.

"I haven't seen the others," Efram says grimly. "We were all separated. I've been put on a working level, gardening."

"Sounds fun," I say.

"Oh, yeah," he says. "I've always wanted to raise asparagus. Time of my life."

I snort then break into full-on laughter at his dry wit. It's not that it's so funny as it is that I really need a good laugh. Efram chuckles too, and then he puts an arm around me and walks us over to the comfy chair I created along with this space. He sits, then pulls me onto his lap. I curl up with him, resting my head on his chest.

We make small talk for a little while, filling the moments with comfortable, understanding silence. He knows what I need better than I do. It's the perfect handling, and it isn't long before I'm feeling more like myself and less like I want to give up.

I lean my head back against his shoulder and look up at his strong jaw, the three-days' growth of his beard scraping my forehead. With a touch on his cheek, I guide his lips to mine and we kiss with a slow, building passion. Gentle, as gentle as Efram's soul.

The soft flames of desire are fanned to life by the exquisite kiss. He gives himself to me, opening the floodgates of his power for me to partake of, drinking my fill. He gives without reservation. In this he's different than all the others. There's always a part of themselves they hold back, consciously or not, but Efram holds nothing back. He's truly an open book with nothing to hide.

"Aviella," Silas voice cuts through our ministrations causing me to jerk around, still in Efram's lap.

"What?" I snap, power gathering around my irritation.

Silas raises his hands defensively and takes a step back.

"I apologize, there is no time," he says. "We have a problem."

I let the power drain away and rise to my feet. Efram stands next to me.

"What is it?" I ask, taking Efram's hand in mine.

"She was here," Silas says.

"She who?" I ask.

Silas' magic betrays his agitation. While his face gives away nothing, his magic is a raging storm. He swallows, bracing himself.

"The enemy," he says. "The one who is behind the Shadow."

"What does that even mean?" I ask.

"It means that we're in trouble," Silas says. "We don't have Rafe or the dragons here. We're down at least four men, and I suspect that there is one other we haven't found yet. But the time is now. It is highly likely that the final showdown could happen here."

"Here?" I ask, stomach dropping to the floor. "Now?"

Numbness creeps through my limbs. I glance at Efram. He's pale, mouth hanging open, and he shakes his head negative.

"Not yet," he says, his voice barely a whisper.

My thoughts race as my heart pounds loud in my ears. This is it. I haven't found my Dad even, but if this is it, then that's all. I'll either win or lose. One way or the other...

"We don't know," Silas says. "We know she was here. She met with He Who Has Risen. We can conjecture that an offer was made. In addition, she's looking for the Power of Twelve."

"What is that?" Efram asks.

Silas gives him the 'don't be a fool' look only Silas can achieve.

"Me," I say, and Silas nods.

"Right," Silas says. "You. He Who Has Risen is looking for you now too. The only question is will he try to take you for himself or give you to her."

"It's a her?" I ask, inhaling deeply and blowing it out. The weight on my shoulders is so heavy it's hard to get a deep breath.

"Yes," Silas says.

"Huh," I say. "Guess all the literature was written by sexist assholes."

I'm rewarded with a rare smile playing across Silas' face. I give him a half-hearted grin back. It's true, though. All the history books and documents have always portrayed the ultimate evil as male. Turns out it's a girl. Or a woman. Or at least looks like one, for now. Maybe she/he can be whatever it wants.

"We're working on a plan," Silas says. "Efram, you need to be ready to react. Nathanial is trying to reach Rafe. I'm reaching out for Tynan and the dragons. We need to extract you from here, now."

"We can't leave without the Innocents," I say.

"We may have to," Silas says.

"No," I shake my head. "We can't."

"Aviella," Silas frowns. "The mages decree is their own, not ours. We cannot allow you to remain at risk here to save them."

"No," I say with my hands on my hips. "It's not their dictate. We're going to need them. I don't know how or why but..."

I trail off because the idea is too big for words. It's an understanding that goes beyond the constraints of language. I throw my hands up in frustration shaking my head.

"Just believe me," I say at last.

"Do you know where they are?" Silas asks.

"Yes," I say, no doubt in my mind. "They're with me, in the lower levels. We need to save every one of them we can."

"I'll tell the others," Silas says.

"Good," I say.

The astral room around us blinks out of existence for an instant then returns stabilizing.

"We've been detected," Efram says. "Avi, let it go. Don't let them catch you here."

"Fine," I say, anger burning my throat with the word. "Work fast, guys. It doesn't sound like we have long."

"We will," Efram and Silas say as I let the astral go, returning to my lonely hard cot.

CHAPTER THIRTY-THREE

AVIELLA

barely slept. All night I couldn't stop thinking about it. This could be it and every time I thought of it, I thought of my Dad. Being tortured, left on his own, and my failure to save him. It was a vicious circle of closed-loop thinking. No escape, all night long, one train of thought following the other.

My eyes are heavy, my footsteps leaden, causing it to take more of my attention than normal to resist the constant barrage of magical suggestions. It'd be so easy to give in. To agree that I too should worship this false prophet like the rest of the poor sheep.

I'm not going back to that. When I get too close to giving in, I glance down the line of the worktable and look at Luca. His face is healing, and he almost looks like himself again. The left side is still swollen, and his normally tan skin is purple with yellow edges from the bruising.

No, I'm not buying into this bullshit. Been there, done that, and have the t-shirt to show for it.

Still the monotony of the work, the droning of the magical coercion, and my overall exhaustion make for one very long stretch of time. My thoughts drift while my hands go through the motions of cleaning the machine parts.

In my head I'm standing in a desert, on a cliff, looking out at stretching sands, cacti and tumbleweeds for as far as the eye can see. Stretching away to the horizon in every direction.

"Hello, Aviella," *a soft, sweet voice says.* "I've been looking for you."

Cold hands grip my heart, and my breath catches in my throat. I don't want to turn around. Fear so strong it's frozen me in place. Behind the fear is the soft buzz of my magic, as if it's been cut off from me. Reaching for it is like touching ice. Shocking cold, so deep it burns.

"What do you want?" *I say, words much more defiant than what I'm feeling.*

Bracing myself, I push through the cold and burning sensation, pull my magic in and wrap myself in it.

"Want?" *she asks.* "It's not what I want, it's what do you want?"

"I want you to stop," *I say, and rage fuels warmth, castigates the fear, leaves me flushing hot.*

"Stop what?" *she asks.* "What have I done?"

"You unleashed war! You've devastated the planet!"

"None of that was me," *she says.*

"Bullshit," *I argue.*

"No," *she says, as I take control of myself enough to turn and face her.*

I'm stunned by her beauty. It's truly beyond compare. She's perfect in every way. Every angle of her body perfection, her face hitting every note so exactly that Leonardo Da Vinci would weep to look upon it and find himself unworthy.

"None of that was me," *she says again, smiling.*

"Then who?" *I snap, resisting the urge to stand and stare.*

"They did this," *she says, motioning with one arm.*

The scene around us shifts, playing through moments in

history. Wars take place in an instant, each one begetting more destruction than the last. Thousands of cars clogging highways, people racing to get nowhere, factories pumping pollution into the air.

"This is their work," she says. "Look on their mighty creations!" Roiling mushroom clouds of smoke and fire climb into the sky in the distance. "How could anything I create compare?"

She's right, of course. Looking on what man has done to man fills me with despair. Maybe there really is no hope for this race and the right answer is to hit the reset button. I waver, for an instant, on the edge of agreeing with her.

But as I watch the atrocities play out around us, my attention being dragged throughout history in an instant, I see something, and for me, it all stops.

A man shielding a child from seeing the explosion in the distance. Protecting the small boy with his own body.

Time rolls back and the scenes replay in reverse. In each moment of tragedy and destruction, there is one, no, hundreds of acts of kindness. Of nobility, of sacrifice.

Sacrifice.

In every single moment, every instance of despair, hundreds if not millions of good people sacrifice themselves for the greater good.

"Aviella, don't you see?" she asks.

"Yes," I agree. "I do."

I turn and face her fully for the first time. Our eyes lock onto each other and her smile falters.

"I do see," I say. "And I think I understand. For the first time it all makes sense now. Thank you."

Her smile fades as the fire in her eyes burns hotter until the beautiful, perfect hazel of them is consumed.

"You will," she growls. "I'll strip away everything you ever loved. You'll watch them all die. Especially this one—"

She motions her hand and we're standing in a clinical, cold operating room. My dad is strapped to the table, struggling.

Screaming in pain as two men work on him with their knives and instruments of torture.

"Dad!" I cry out.

"No," she says, the scene fading away. "Not yet. Soon, though. He's waiting for you. I'll make sure he lives long enough for you to hold him while he dies. Trust me, I'm good at this."

"NO!" I scream.

"NO!" I'm screaming. Then the pain hits and I drop to the ground, unable to control my body.

"NO!" Aviella screams, jerking away from the worktable.

The red-robed guards react in an instant, and she drops to the ground as hundreds of volts race through her body. She's convulsing in reaction. I can't let this happen. Leaping to my feet I race to her side. Her teeth are chattering, and her eyes are rolling back up in her head.

I don't know what happened, but I'm not going to let her suffer like this. The red-robed guards hit me with their clubs, but I soften the blows with magic. Bracing myself, I grab Aviella. The electricity coursing through her transfers to me. I grit my teeth and work through the pain, passing it through my body and into the ground, guiding it with magic.

She stops convulsing, going still. I touch her throat, checking for a pulse, and find one. It's weak, thready, but there. An instant later, all my magic is sucked away, and the blows raining down on me make full contact.

I drop to the ground and curl up around her the best I can, protecting her with my body as the darkness closes in.

I'm barely aware as we're both lifted and carried out of

the room. My consciousness skips moments of time with mini blackouts as I struggle to remain aware. I can sense my magic—it's out there, but I can't reach it. A barrier is between me and it.

They throw us roughly into a side room. We land in a pile together and they turn to leave. Two of the guards stand in the door looking at us.

"I think one of them should be it," one says to the other.

"Yeah, they're both trouble-makers," his partner says. "Give them both up for all I care."

"Flip a coin?"

"I'm sure He Who Has Risen knows which one is to go."

"Right. All is clear to him, praise be his name."

They walk out and slam the door. I focus on breathing so I can disentangle myself from her enough to check her over. The block on my magic has been lifted, so I flow a trickle of healing energy into her. Nothing too much, though the desire is strong to flood her with it and heal her completely. If I did that, their alarms would trigger, and we'd both suffer more for it.

She stirs, eyelids fluttering, then she gasps and jerks upright. Her eyes are wide, breath rapid, and sweat beads her forehead as she looks around.

"Where is she?" Aviella asks.

"Who?" I ask.

"Her! The enemy, she was…" she trails off, pulling her knees up to her chest and hugging them tight. "Oh."

I scoot in close and wrap my arms around her. She rests her head against my chest. We sit in silence for a long time but there is nowhere for us to be, and nothing else I would rather be doing, though I wish the circumstances were different.

When she pulls herself out of my arms and sits up straight, she's composed. She wipes the sweat away with the sleeve of her jumper, straightens her hair, and sighs heavily before giving me a half smile.

"It's fine," she says.

"Is it?" I ask, trying to gauge the truth of her words.

"Yeah," she says. "I think I've met my enemy."

"I see," I say. "How was that?"

"Oh, you know, tea and cakes. Good times for all."

"Glad to hear it," I say, my stomach churning.

Something in her eyes has grown colder, resolved might be the best I can call it. She's displaying a certainty that wasn't there before, which is good, but it also makes me sad.

"I know what it's going to take," she says softly. "This isn't going to be easy."

"Is it ever?" I ask, and she smiles.

"I guess not," she says, squaring her shoulders and dropping her knees from her chest. "It's fine, though. Remember that, will you? Let the others know."

"Aviella," I say, stomach sinking. "You're scaring me."

It's a harsh thing to admit, but I don't know how else to phrase it. There's a finality to her words. She touches my cheek.

"It will all be okay," she says. "We're going to do what we have to do. All of us."

"Okay," I agree. I put my arm around her shoulders and lean my back against the wall to wait.

I'm not sure what she's planning, but it can't be good. I'll have to get with the others and see what we can do to help. If nothing else, I've found the Innocents my brothers and I were looking for. Now if we can figure out a way to save them.

CHAPTER THIRTY-FIVE

SILAS

"*I* know she's here," He Who Has Risen says, his voice almost hissing. It grates on my nerves. "I know it's a girl. I know this much for sure. What I don't know is which one!"

"That is a problem," I observe, keeping my emotions separate and observing the scene.

"Right?" he muses, pacing the length of his office. He rubs his chin thoughtfully. "Historian, how do I find her?"

"Why do you want to?" I ask.

He stops in his tracks but doesn't turn.

"Why do I want to?" he asks, speaking softly. "Why do I want to?"

"It seems a logic—"

"Because SHE want her!" he screams, turning, his face an apoplectic purple. "If SHE wants her, then you bet your damn fine shoes that means there's power to be had there. Power that I need to control, not her."

"I see," I say, unflinching.

"No," he seethes. "No, you don't. Only I have seen God's face and been granted the ability to see the truth. You know how hard it is to hold out against Her? I can't allow her an advantage, and She wants this one bad. She doesn't appear in person often."

"I will do what I can," I say noncommittally.

"See that you do," he says, a grin on his face. "Use all your powers, Historian. All of them, do you understand me?"

A cold chill trickles down my spine as his eyes bore into me. I swallow hard and nod.

"Of course," I say, backing out of the room.

The smile on his face is enough for me to judge the man crazy, then when you talk to him . . . well, that seals the deal, doesn't it?

The instant the door is closed, I breathe a sigh of relief, then turn and run, ignoring the guards and the assistants who barely give me a glance anyway. They're used to people running from the head man's office, apparently.

As I run, I reach out for Efram. Nathanial is working security. I can't go to him for help because there will be too many eyes around. Efram is my best hope. My awareness stretches until I sense him two floors below.

I take the stairs down three at a time, leaping down to each landing and vaulting to the next stairs. When I reach the floor he is on, I stop and compose myself. When my breathing is under control, I open the door and step out.

Hydroponic gardens stretch for as far as the eye can see. UV Lights hang over the growing gardens and workers move up and down the line, tending and harvesting the plants. A guard steps in front of me, an automatic weapon held across his body.

He hawks, turns his head and spits. "No entry."

"I am the Historian," I say, pulling out my identification and flashing it before his eyes.

His eyes glaze over, and he returns to his post next to the door. My credentials aren't what's letting me through, it's magic, of course. The flashing of the credentials was merely a cover to help his mind build a story for why he let me pass.

I close my eyes to orient myself magically to the room and my relationship to where Efram is, then take off down one of the long rows. I find him bent over a plant, pulling death energy from some of its dead leaves so that the rest of it might live.

"Delicate work," I observe, and he jumps, banging his head on the pipe that carries water down the line.

"Silas!" he gasps.

"Efram," I say.

"What are you doing here? You can't be here, they're going to take us both!"

"It's fine," I assure him. "For a few minutes, we have a problem."

"A problem?" I ask.

"He knows about Aviella," I say.

"What? How?" Efram asks, immediately grasping the situation.

"Apparently our enemy came and made herself known," I say.

"Her?" Efram asks. "I thought it was a He."

"That's rather sexist isn't it?" I ask.

"No, I mean, all the pictures…" He stutters and stumbles, then stops when he realizes I was being humorous. It's a common enough mistake after all. "We have to get her out of here."

"Yes," I agree. "Problem is, we don't have backup yet. I can't reach Tynan or Rafe."

"Shit," Efram says, looking around to make sure none of the guards are coming. "Can you and I form a gate without them?"

"I don't think so," I say. "Unless you have a key I don't know about?"

He shakes his head negative. He's shaking in anger or frustration or perhaps a mix, I don't know which.

"How do we get her out of here?" he asks.

"I'll try to reach outside," I say. "Luca is down there with her. Have you been able to talk to her through the astral?"

"Yes," he says. "Briefly."

"Okay, good," I say. "As soon as you're off shift, reach out to her. I'm being watched too closely and so is Nathanial. Give her a heads up. If you can reach Luca too, that'd be good."

"Right," he says. "What about the Innocents? The mages aren't going to want to leave them behind."

I grimace because he's right. Shaking my head, I shrug.

"Aviella is our priority. I have to go," I say, turning but I stop before leaving. "Efram, make sure you let her know. I don't want her in the dark on this."

"Of course," he says, frowning. "It won't be easy, but I can do it."

"Good," I say. "We'll figure this out. We need to get her out of here by tomorrow before they get any bright ideas."

"What if we can't?" he asks, speaking so softly I barely hear him.

"That's not an option," I say before striding away.

CHAPTER THIRTY-SIX

NATHANIAL

*T*he call is unexpected, sudden, but there is no doubt of it. I'm sitting, watching the monitors when it happens. A touch, lighter than a feather, and the restraints on me fall away. Divine grace drifts through me like a leaf drifting on a gentle breeze. Light and airy, lifting me up.

It's time.

How this can be the time makes no sense to me, but this is it, and I am but an instrument of the will of the Divine. I rise to my feet.

"Hey, where are you going?" Richard asks, looking up from his fat belly, gravy dribbling down both of his chins.

"I must attend an errand," I say.

"Oh, I get it, you gots to go, bathroom, right?" he asks.

"Something like that," I say, letting him make of my words what he will.

"Yeah, those urges hit me sometimes too, real bad like," he nods sagely.

"I'm sure they do," I say, biting off my further thoughts on his bodily functions or mis-functions, as would be a more appropriate statement.

Turning before he can say more, I leave the security office. Outside, the hall is filled with people, believers as they call themselves. They don't believe, they're all followers of a false prophet. It breaks my heart. The entire bunker is decorated with false idols of He Who Has Risen. They don't see it and for the most part, they can't. What did they have left to believe in when the world came to an end?

These are the ones who were already lost when it came. Self-entitled, enamored only with the things they could touch or feel and having lost all sense of the Divine. No belief left that there was something more than the life they were living and their constant pursuit of immediate pleasures.

The enemy worked her plan well, smart. The constant pressures of their lives from before left them lost and vulnerable. Now with the magical reinforcement that He Who Has Risen is the one, subtly whispering to them that he must be followed and obeyed, is it any wonder they do? They're prepared for this by their entire prior lives.

Bracing myself to walk amongst them, I do the only thing I can—I ignore them. I cannot allow myself to fall into the depth of despair they carry inside of themselves. My own nature would demand of me that I help them, and now is not the time. I cling to my unlocked purpose, reaching out through the astral for Aviella. She is my anchor.

Privacy. It's a hard, almost impossible thing to come by here. My quarters are the only option I have, so I race through the halls to them. I know, very well, that even here in my quarters, I am watched. They tried to hide the fact that they do, but their attempts were feeble. It doesn't matter though, those watching will only see me meditating.

I sit on the bed, cross legged, and close my eyes. I flow

myself out of this mortal coil and seek Aviella on the spiritual plane. The astral, as the others would call it.

"Nate?" she asks, looking up in surprise.

"Yes," I answer, closing with her and wrapping my arms around her tightly.

She cuddles up against my chest without hesitation. The most beautiful thing about her, she holds nothing back. There is no reservation to her. She loves freely, deeply, and with a profound truth. Her magic rises, flowing around and embracing the two of us.

My own magic blends to hers and on that level, we become one.

"This sucks," she whispers.

"I know," I say. "You've done well."

"Have I? How do I save these people Nate? They're lost. I feel it in them, their despair, their need for something, anything to believe in."

Having no answer, I run my fingers through her hair and down her spine. Here she is beautiful as always. There are no signs of the abuse she's been dealt. She shivers, pulling me tighter. She looks up with a sparkle in her eyes and a smile playing across her lips.

She rises onto her toes and touches her lips gently to mine...

CHAPTER THIRTY-SEVEN

AVIELLA

I'm so happy he's here that I throw myself into him. I keep my body on the physical plane, making the necessary motions, cleaning the parts of machines I don't even begin to understand, but in the astral, I kiss Nate. His lips are soft and lovely. A thrill runs through me at their touch, igniting desire.

Pulling him tighter I want to meld our two bodies together. The two of us to become one here on some spiritual level, but that isn't possible, no matter how much I want it. We can join though, if he's ready to give in to me.

Is he?

Pulling back from the kiss I stare into his eyes searching for an answer. My answer comes when he squeezes my ass and lifts me up to meet his lips again. His hard cock digs into my middle, and now the kiss turns sweet to passionate.

Desire instantly becomes an inferno consuming all my thoughts. I lose myself in the pleasures of his touches as they wash away the pain and suffering I've been enduring. His magic and his arms are warmth, comfort, embracing me in safety and relief.

The passion of the kiss grows, filled with desire and pent-up need. Something in him has changed, as he doesn't pull back but gives himself to me in full. His mouth on mine is insistent, demanding as his tongue invades my mouth.

His hands move over my body, and I melt against him.

Here in the astral it responds easier to my thoughts and desires than reality. A bed forms behind us, and he senses it. Turning, he drops us onto it, his muscular form covering me. A shimmer behind him catches my attention as I catch glimpses of his wings. He normally has them hidden or dismissed, or whatever it is angels do with their wings when they want to appear normal. They're not fully here, but I see the outlines of them, so golden they almost appear white.

In my magical sight, he pulses with energy, pure, clearly Divine in nature. I've always known that Nate was powerful, but he's kept the full depths and heights and range of his power hidden from me before now.

The thrill of his unleashed power flowing through me, stroking my skin, mingling with my own magic is ecstatic. Twining my fingers in his hair I jerk his head back and stare into his eyes. Grinding my hips against his hard cock so that he groans.

"Avi," he says, his voice a hoarse whisper.

He jerks his head forward to crush my lips. He bites my lower lip, pulling on it and thrusts his fully clothed hips against mine.

His fingers run through my hair, magic through my soul, and then he's undressing me. He pulls my shirt over my head and tosses it then rises up so he can pull off my pants.

As he slides them down over my ass he stops and his eyes drink me in, filled with lust and admiration. Leaning in, he kisses down my neck, between my breasts, working his way lower.

Rising onto my elbows I stop him. The look of disappointment on his face is almost comical if it wasn't so sincere. Shaking a finger before him I smile.

"Clothes," I say, looking down at him.

He smiles and stands up. Slowly he unbuttons his shirt, revealing those rock-hard muscles underneath. As the shirt drops to the ground, his wings shimmer into existence, and there's a golden glow around him. He undoes his belt, slowly opening the fly of his pants.

The massive bulge in his underwear clearly states his readiness. He lets the pants slide down and hooks his fingers under the band of his underwear. Who knew uptight Nate would be such a showman when it came to the bedroom?

His slow teasing is making me hotter though. I love the reveal of his muscles, and now he slowly slides the underwear out and over the head of his cock. It's so hard it's purple, ready to explode with his desire.

I slide my hand down across my stomach and lightly stroke my clit while watching him undress. A shiver races through me as his cock drops free, and I slide a finger inside myself at the same time. His cock bounces, ready to be satisfied.

He climbs back on the bed, positioning his dick so he's ready to go.

He kisses me, his arms resting to either side of my head. His tongue teases at my lips slowly parting them. As the kiss deepens, he thrusts his cock, balls deep, in a single driving force.

I cry out in pleasure and surprise.

As he drives into me, our magical powers escalate. A storm of pure magical energy forms around us, escalating in ways I've not yet experienced.

I drink him in, taking his power that he freely offers, absorbing it into mine.

He thrusts, and I meet each forward push. The pleasures

of my flesh match the swirls of magic building. His hands are everywhere. He's touching me in places and ways I can't comprehend. I'm a tingling ball of sensations all over.

The magic goes higher still, and suddenly inside of me, everything is shifting. Reservoirs of power I didn't know I had open up, and I'm pounding with it. It's too much to contain. The power is building too far.

"Nate!" I cry out his name as he slams into me again and again.

Suddenly I'm there, falling into the orgasm and when I do, I can't hold back the magic either. It explodes. Power engulfing us, and then firing into the sky like a giant spotlight, highlighting the place where we've joined.

I'm out of my body, watching it all from above. Waves of powerful pleasure passing over and through me as I watch Nate collapse onto me. He's kissing my neck and cheek. It's sweet and gentle. Nate, through and through.

I snuggle up next to him to bask in his warmth, hiding from my harsh reality. I'm painfully aware of it, but being here in the astral, with him, keeps it separate. It hurts less, it's more distant, and I'm able to pretend it's not me, if only for a little while.

Nate wraps his arm around my shoulders, holding me tight against him, silent and strong, sensing my need for comfort.

"I love you," he says, his heart beating strong beneath my ear.

It's an admission for him. One he's been avoiding confronting, which I sense through the connection we have. A connection that is now even stronger. His magic is part and parcel of who I am now, which means he is too.

He's been conflicted, struggling to contain his feelings. No, it's more than that. I send magical energy into him, information flowing to me easily along our channels, and as I do, I'm opening myself to him too. He isn't locking anything away, he's sharing all he is with me, and I do the same.

"I know," I say softly. "I love you, Nate."

His conflict is between his heart and duty. As I touch on it, the concepts he deals in are so far beyond anything I've considered, I can't wrap my mind around them. His nature is defined by the Divine. He is an instrument of Divine will, first and foremost, for millennia untold. Until me.

When with me is the first time he's ever questioned. Ever wondered. Ever dreamt of something more than blind obedience.

His power pulses in me, part of me, and my touch is in him. He's mine just as much as any of the guys are. They're all mine, part of me, helping me to become…. What?

The savior I need to be?

The idea is less daunting than it's ever been. There has to be some reason for all I've been through. All the death, the loss, the torments of what I've seen, and more, what I've done. The weight of the fall of Tynan's bunker and those I couldn't save lies heavy on my heart. And through it all what theme?

Sacrifice.

It's coming. I know it's coming. Every turn in the road is another choice. One I have to make, each time. They'll all look to me, and eventually…

Nate kisses me, stopping the dark turn of my thoughts. I throw my leg over his, pressing myself closer, and lose myself in this moment. Taking what small pleasures I can, as his manhood rises to service once more.

CHAPTER THIRTY-EIGHT

NATHANIAL

*L*eaving her is the hardest thing I've done in my existence. She's in pain, physically and spiritually. I can't stay, though. It will only cause more pain. If I held her here in the astral, with me, her body would suffer.

"You must go back," I say.

"I know," she says, not lifting her head from my chest.

She's running her fingers over my chest and stomach, light touches that almost tickle. She sighs in resignation but doesn't rise.

"I do not want you to," I admit.

"I know," she says, looking up with a smile that lights her eyes.

She hesitates only a moment longer then draws upon the depths of strength that I remain in awe of. She rises onto an elbow, looking into my eyes, then she puts on a stoic face with a half-smile—but this time it doesn't touch her eyes. It's a lie, blatant and obvious, but one she is doing for me.

"It won't be much longer," I say.

"Yeah," she laughs. "It's all coming to a head, isn't it?"

Grimacing, I nod. "Yes. The enemy is growing bolder."

Aviella nods before climbing to her feet, and with a thought she is dressed, covering the Divine beauty of her naked form. I can't keep the disappointment from my face.

"Twice, Nate," she laughs. "It's enough.... For now." she says, her voice and eyes filled with promises for the future. My cock stiffens once more at her words and part of my thoughts spin off into imagination of all the ways we can partake of the pleasures of flesh. I return her smile then kiss her softly as she fades out of the astral, leaving me alone.

Surprisingly, her absence hurts. I'm sending her into a lion's den alone. Even Daniel had one of my brothers to watch over him when he entered the den, but Aviella walks alone. It's not fair. Why?

The black maw of doubt opens. I've never experienced this. The Divine is separate, I reach for it, but the darkness blocks me. The Divine has always been there, it's part of me, I am a creature of it by nature. In all my long existence, I've never doubted.

Is this what happened to her? Is this what she faced? If one as great as her fell to this, then what hope is there?

Aviella is suffering. It's wrong. I can stop it. Jumping to my feet, hands clenching into fists, magic becoming a storm I step towards the door. I can save her.

I know, though, this isn't the path. I stop, standing at this terrible crossroads. Torn by this decision. I can save her. If I reached out to the others, we'd tear this place apart. She'd be safe. We'd whisk her away. Away from all of this.

The eleven of us could create a safe haven where we could protect her from the world. Imagination spins out the scenario in my mind. Aviella, happy. Cared for in every way possible. Let the world outside burn. Rafe and I together, with the aid of the mages and Tynan, could create a pocket reality. Leave all the survivors to their fate.

Let the Shadow have this existence.

We could…

Aviella's pain calls to me. Demands I stop it. I can save her. I know it's not my path to do so, is not the will of the Divine. But what if the Divine is wrong? Why must it always be a choice of sacrifices?

The path of martyrs is long and bloody. We could save her from the pain and ravages it will bring. I've never faced a choice like this. My obedience to the will of the Divine has been absolute. I sink onto the bed knowing I have to make a choice. Which fork in the road do I follow?

Do I save Aviella at the cost of the world itself? Or do I keep my faith in the Divine?

viella.

    A soft voice calls my name, calling me. I'm asleep but not, in some strange state where I'm above my sleeping body looking down on it there on the hard bed. Turning, or the equivalent feeling of turning, my attention is drawn to a golden light. As I watch, it grows brighter and brighter. It's warm and welcoming and feels... nurturing.

Who is it? I ask, drawing closer to the light, or more accurately, pulled to it.

There isn't an answer in words, but there is a response from the light. It's pure, so pure and soft and warm and so many other adjectives yet none of them encompass the essence of it. I'm drawn into the light and surrounded by it. Embraced, closer to whole than I've ever felt in my life.

The world is softly golden, taking on shape around me. I'm still not my body, but a projection into the astral. My actual body is back in the living hell that is the lowest floors of New Jerusalem, sleeping. Astral projecting I get, but this is different. I'm not an astral body, I'm something simpler, purer. I'm me.

Aware of myself and my surroundings. It's an odd sensation, and I take a few moments to revel in the freedom. It's freeing and powerful. In a way that's all I am right now, potential for power. The depths of reserves unlocking in me are beyond anything I'd ever imagined.

As the space around me takes form, a shape comes before me. It's indistinct. In every aspect, it is light given the idea of a shape, more than an actual shape.

Oh my dear Avi...

The light-shape thing touches my cheek, and the glow of its touch ignites deep memories. Warmth floods my being as they rush forward from the depths of time, it can't be....

Mom? I ask.

The light shape smiles but doesn't answer. Tears would be streaming down my face if I had eyes.

I know how hard this has been, she says. *Know I love you, more than anything. The pain is temporary, I will be with you the entire way. The sacrifice you must make will be hard, but I will carry you through,* she says.

Mom, I can't. How do I? How do I choose? I ask.

You will know.

The light is gone as suddenly as it hit and I'm back in my body, alone, lying on the hard bunk. Rolling into a ball I pull my knees up to my chest and let the tears flow.

I don't want to choose. This is going to hurt, and there's no way to avoid it. I'm going to lose them. One of them or all of them, I don't know yet. I can only hope they hold strong. My dear, brave boys. I love them all, and I know this is going to tear them apart.

CHAPTER FORTY

SILAS

Finally, I trace the last symbol on the wall. They create a loop in the security cameras so they won't see what I'm doing. I reach out to Nathanial to be sure it worked.

It is working, he responds, watching the monitor.

Good. Now for the real work.

Once I'm sitting down cross legged, I clear my thoughts and find the deep focus I'll need for this. As my breathing evens out and my heart rate slows, I'm able to reach out of myself, searching across the astral.

New Jerusalem is built of barriers that block magic in and out. As I navigate my way through the symbols that form the magic, it's obvious why the mages couldn't find the Innocents that are here. Glowing blue signs dance around as I study each in turn. As I gain an understanding of each one, I know how to circumvent it, and another piece of the barrier falls.

I've been working on this for days with Nathanial's help. I've almost done enough that I should be able to contact Rafe, the dragons, and the mages. It's tedious work requiring infinite patience, but if my long life has given me no other gifts, this I have learned in abundance.

A new barrier appears as the one I'm working on fades. This one has a purple glow and scripts from ancient Babylon. The level of work and detail is far and above anything that the false prophet could construct himself. There is no doubt he's being helped, but by whom?

This one takes more time. I work on it for hours, during most of the night, until at last I'm able to reach through it without setting off any alarms. I reach out for the others, forming a meeting place inside the barriers. Rafe appears first.

"Where is she?" Rafe asks.

"Patience," I counsel, reaching for the rest.

Killian, Gavin, and Ronan appear almost simultaneously, and before they speak, Nathanial and Luca join us. They speak over each other, but I ignore them. We all have to be here, so I reach out further, stretching to the limits of my own power.

There...

Tynan appears and brings with him a storm of raging emotions. He stands imperiously, looking at those assembled with a haughty arrogance only he could manage. Shen and Alaric appear behind him, flanking their brother. Silence falls across even this headstrong group of men as he gazes on each of us.

"We're here," I say, shifting my feet as his gaze lands on me.

"So I see," Tynan says. "Why have you risked this?"

"Because I needed it," Aviella says.

All of us turn at the sound of her voice. My blood runs hot as desire and needs beyond compare ignite in her presence. It's clear I'm not the only one that she has this effect on.

"Aviella, this is very risky," Tynan says. "There are forces to bear here beyond anything you can comprehend."

"Is that right?" she asks, tilting her head and focusing on him. "Really?"

Tynan shuts up for probably the first time in his entire existence. I can't suppress a grin.

"Aviella," Efram says, stepping forward. "They're watching all of us. This is really dangerous."

She smiles at Efram, walking over to him and placing her fingers on his cheek. They stare into each other's eyes for a long moment while all of us watch, waiting.

"I know," she says. She inhales slowly then exhales and the astral space changes. A long table laden with food appears. "I need you. All of you."

She turns her attention from Efram and looks at each of us in turn. As her gaze lands on me I sense the weight on her shoulders. Her lips tremble and there are unshed tears in the corners of her eyes, but nothing else reveals the pressure she's under.

"We need this," she says, turning and motioning to the food. "It's only for a little while. A small escape, let's eat."

"This isn't wise," Tynan says.

"Aviella, the Shadow is moving, marching on this bunker, right now," Rafe says. "I've been trying to get in here to warn you, but they've put up new wards."

"I know," she sighs, turning to Rafe.

She walks over and rises onto her toes, hooking her hands behind his head and pulling him down into a deep and passionate kiss. No one says anything more as Aviella ushers us to the table with a motion. We take places along the table, naturally falling into an unspoken pecking order. I doubt the other men notice, but a long life of being an observer makes it interesting to me.

Tynan claims her right-hand side, and Efram goes to her

left. Rafe takes a seat beside Tynan while Nathanial sits beside Efram. The balancing of forces, the strength of personalities, and the roles we each play to her lay out in the simple procedure of sitting down to a meal.

The four mages take Nathanial's side while Alaric and Shen sit beside Rafe. Left standing I move to sit next to Shen. Aviella stands up and looks down the length of our table, at the eleven of us. There are not twelve... yet, but there's an empty seat next to me as if she knows there should be.

"This journey," she says, holding a cup in both of her hands, staring into the liquid it contains. "Has been long, hard, and I can't tell you each how much you all mean to me. I wouldn't have made it through this without you."

"This sounds an awful lot like a goodbye," Rafe says.

"It's not," she says, shaking her head. "But it is time we acknowledge what we face."

"The leader of the Shadow has been revealed," Nathanial says.

"Yeah," Aviella sighs, her shoulders bowing. "She has, and it's not good, but then what else could we possibly expect? The world has literally gone to hell."

She laughs and shakes her head. It's not a joyful laughter, but one filled with pain and loss.

"We can face this," Efram says, placing a hand on her hip.

"Sure," she agrees. "And win or lose, we will."

"We will win," Tynan says, his voice every bit as dominant as his personality. Deep, rich and certain of himself.

"Maybe. I've learned so much, from each of you. I wanted to do this," she motions at the table laden with food and drinks she created with her magic, "as a thank-you."

"Aviella, none of this is necessary," Tynan says standing next to her. He puts his arm around her waist and looks up and down the table meeting each of our eyes. "All of us are here for you. We will follow you unto the ends of the earth."

She looks up at him and I'm barely at an angle where I can see the sadness on her face if not her eyes. She smiles, but it's the smile of a clown. Laughing to keep from crying.

"Right," she says. "Dig in, please. I know it's 'fake' being all here on the astral but as it is, we can't all meet in person, can we? So take this small gift and partake of it. I want to give each of you some of my magic, as you've all given yours to me. I want to share this with you."

There is no more need for words or speeches. There is light discussion as we fall to eating. The table is too long for easy conversation to reach one end to the other leaving me caught as judge for Alaric and Shen as they discuss the fine art of hunting trumpet beasts. The two dragons are deep into a game of one-upmanship between each other about their hunting.

I, for my part, have zero interest in any of it, but there is an old standing rule about never pissing off a dragon, so I play along. I'm not a fool, after all. Mostly, though, I watch. Especially Aviella.

It doesn't escape me how she looks at each of us in turn with long, sad looks that make me wonder what is happening in her thoughts. She's never been like this, uncertain yet resigned. I partake lightly of the food without much thought, but even the tastes of it carry hints of melancholy.

As the dining comes to an end, Aviella stands again.

"Guys," she says. "Thank you. So much. There are hard choices to be made, and I will make them. I'll have to, but each of you mean the world to me. If anyone..." she chokes up and wipes a tear away from her eye. Tynan and Efram both leap to their feet, tangling with each other as they put an arm around her.

Surprisingly, Efram holds his ground, refusing to move for Tynan. Power builds for an instant as the two men pull magic to them, ready to battle over her but she touches their cheeks, both at the same time without looking up. The magic drains away and the two of them work it out peacefully in an instant.

The power she wields, not even in terms of raw magical power, the power she has over our hearts and minds is absolute. It's incredible to watch in action, and I'm astute enough to know that I am not exempt from her charms.

She turns her back to Tynan and leans against Efram, her head resting on his shoulder. It almost looks like she's whispering something to him, and to add to my guess his face turns pale. His jaw tightens, and his eyes narrow.

She straightens, squares her shoulders, drops her arms to her sides and then grabs a drink off the table. After taking a long sip she grips the chalice tightly in her hands then chuckles.

"I guess that's it," she says, shaking her head. "No matter what happens, remember, I love you. I can't ask any more of any of you. You've all done your parts, now it's up to me."

"I do not agree with this, Aviella," Tynan says. "None of us do. We are with you to the end."

"That's sweet," she says, shaking her head. "Our enemy is subtle, smart, and deadly. No matter what, remember, okay?"

"Of course," all of us murmur our agreement.

"I've got to go back," she says. The table and chairs fade away as she lets her magic go. "I am in each of you now, and you are each in me. Forever."

She fades away, leaving the astral and the eleven of us staring at each other.

CHAPTER FORTY-ONE

AVIELLA

"*I*dle hands are the devil's playthings," the Inquisitor says, marching up and down the line. "You must learn that being productive is for your own good. Hard work, the pain of the flesh cleanses the soul."

"Yes,, Inquisitor," we intone as we've been beaten into doing.

The Inquisitor visits our floor at least once a week. Or more. I don't know, it all blurs together. He comes, and he preaches, and we listen or take our beatings. I'm convinced it's random who will take the abuse. There's no rhyme or reason to any of it. You believe, at first, that if you obey the rules, it won't happen to you. That's a lie. A lie to get you comfortable, so you don't expect it when it comes.

"Rise up!" he yells.

We stand, some of us slower than others. A lot of the people down here are old. Or they look old, at least. Broken. Keeping my head down, I glance in each direction, looking at those trapped here with me. They don't have the escapes I do. They don't get to go to the astral and be comforted by their lovers. Each of them is on their own, and the fact that they're still going at all is a testament to their willpower.

The red-robed guards march down the line and hit three different people with their taser batons. Those hit drop onto the table, convulsing under the electric current. Gritting my teeth, I force my hands to unclench. I could take them all out. Unbidden, my power swells, pushing its way up, ready for use, and I barely manage to hold it back.

Luca's magic is a feather's touch against mine. He shakes his head, mouthing a no. As if I don't know how bad it would be for me to let loose. I'm not a killer and these people, as evil as they seem, aren't. I know evil. I've felt it, been face to face with it, and even the Inquisitor at the front of the room doesn't make the grade.

They're stupid, sure. Misguided and lost, but they're all struggling. Trying to understand the world they've unknowingly created. Working to survive. No matter how much they piss me off, they're not evil. That doesn't mean I won't beat them senseless though. That might teach them a lesson.

I close my eyes to better push aside the anger and the despair that follows behind it. The path I must walk stretches out before me. It's a decision. The choice is mine, which in itself is really a Divine joke, isn't it? Free will, but what is free will when the options before you are terrible? Bad, and then even worse, make your choice.

The girl ahead of me screams in pain as they continue using the shock sticks. The Inquisitor is droning on about the need to be cleansed. The magical pressure to comply, obey, that this is normal, pushes against me with a beat of its own, almost in time with my heart.

Anger boils. Rage. The crying sets my teeth on edge. I can stop this. I should stop this.

It takes a sacrifice. There is no doubt, and the dream of my mom comes unbidden. I don't know if it was real, but it felt like it. As real as an astral meeting with the boys, but still different. Is she with me?

Doubts claw my thoughts, but the anger burns them away and I'm left with resolve.

"PLEASE! STOP!" the girl being beaten cries out.

She's huddled in a ball on the ground, and still they continue. Everything slows, then each piece of the room becomes a still photograph. A frozen moment in time as I look at each one. Unconsciously, I take a step forward.

Luca reaches for me. I see his hand moving, but he's too slow. This is the path.

I am with you Aviella, my mother's presence echoes through my thoughts.

"Stop," I say, my voice barely a whisper.

They don't. Their arms rise and fall, thrusting forward, and her cries have reduced to whimpers. In my magical sight, the flame of her life force is flickering. She can't take much more. She's going to give up.

"Stop!" I yell, the word tearing its way out of my throat.

When I raise my fists, they're glowing bright white. Power pulses through me. The guards turn. Their eyes widen as their mouths drop open, and the first glimmers of fear appear on their faces.

I'll teach them fear.

"This is not the way," I say.

"Aviella, no!" Luca shouts.

"Unclean! Stop her!" the High Inquisitor yells.

The guards hesitate, but step forward, raising their prods. I form magic into a shielding cloak, pulling more power to me. It flows in from each of my boys as I draw on them as well as my own reserves. This is it; my path has led me to this moment. The choice is before me, and I've made it.

It's the only way to stop the madness. They want a sacrifice, well I'm going to give them one. The guard's arm arcs up and over, swinging down at the poor girl. I grab his forearm before he can finish the motion. He turns his head, surprise in his eyes, but even more so when I flip him over by that same arm, and he slams against the ground, hard.

Two more guards race towards me. A wave of my hand, and they're flying through the air to slam against the walls. I stride down the length of the room towards the High Inquisitor. He's watching with a maniacal grin on his face. I'm going to punch that fucking grin right off of it.

I kneel beside the girl on the floor without taking my eyes off the High Inquisitor. I lay my hands on her. My hands glow white as I push magic into body. It's cold as her own latent magic climbs in response to mine. She stops convulsing and her heart slows, stabilizing.

I stand up and stare at the High Inquisitor. He points a long gnarly finger at me. "Unclean."

"You're damn straight," I growl. "This is over. I'm done with this game."

Luca is right behind me, putting a hand on my shoulder.

"Avi," he says. "Don't—"

I jerk my shoulder free of his restraint and charge the Inquisitor. The magic pulses in time with the beating of my heart. I'm going to break us all out of here. I'm setting this bunker free, and I'm doing it right now.

Balling my hands into fists I raise my right hand and swing as if I'm going to punch the Inquisitor, using it as a focus for the magic. The force explodes from my swinging fist, racing towards the grinning asshole. He pulls something from inside his robe and holds it up in front of himself. I don't expect it to do anything, it looks like a metal rod about the size of a soda can but twice as long.

The rod intercepts the speeding magical force bolt, and the bolt splits harmlessly around it. Doors open around the long room in which we're kept, and dozens of guards dressed in red robes race through.

"Aviella!" Luca yells.

He's throwing magic around freely. The air around me thrums with his power too. Turning in circles, I wield my own magic and fight the incoming guards. They keep coming, practically climbing over each other in their eagerness to fight.

There are too many. I can't keep them all back or even in sight. Blows rain down on my body, breaking through my magical shields, hitting me over and over. Some of them are wielding stunners that send shocks of electricity through my body. It's affecting my ability to control the magical flow.

Suddenly something clamps on my neck.

It's cold, hard, so tight it's almost choking, and as it snaps shut, the magic is gone. I can feel it, but there's a wall between me and it. I can't reach it or pull it in more than a tiny trickle. When I do my neck becomes an inferno that races through my limbs, and I cry out in pain.

I drop to my knees as they continue to assault me, beating and kicking me from all sides. When it stops at last, my mouth is filled with blood and I can barely keep my eyes open. A pair of black, pointy boots step into my limited field of vision. The Inquisitor kneels in front of me, grabbing my chin and jerking my head up to look at his face.

"Well, well," he says. "He Who Has Risen is going to be so happy to see you at last."

"F... u," I can't form the words, the pain is too great. I'm fairly sure that my jaw is broken too. Every breath is sharp, stabbing pain telling me I've broken ribs too.

"Bring her," he orders, and I black out as they jerk me off the floor.

CHAPTER FORTY-TWO

LUCA

*T*hey overwhelmed her, and I couldn't do a damn thing about it. There were too many of them. Why didn't she listen to me?

The cold-iron collar around my neck burns as I do my best to ignore it. It's a constant ache that I want to recoil from, but there is no escape. Water drips steadily somewhere, echoing around the five by five room they've shoved me into. No mattress or creature comforts. They don't even bother with a chamber pot.

When they hauled me down, I was barely conscious. Still, I know that Aviella is in the room next to mine, but I can't reach her. All I can do is listen and wait to hear her wake up and contemplate what else I could have done to save her.

We should have pulled her out of here faster. It's not like we don't know how volatile she is when she sees others suffering. She can't control her instinct to help. That very instinct is what draws us to her. Pulls me to her.

In all my years walking this earth I've only known one other who comes close to her, but even Joan could never compare to Aviella. Her selflessness is without bounds. She truly takes on the suffering of all around her and in so doing she lightens their pain.

"Ugh," Aviella groans.

"Aviella!" I leap to the door, pressing my face against the rough wood and peering out the small barred window.

"Yeah," she says.

"How badly are you hurt?" I ask.

"On a scale of one to ten?" she asks. "About a fifteen."

"I'm sorry," I say. "Silas and Nathanial will get us out of here. We have to be patient."

She doesn't answer. I wait and seconds tick by until I'm left wondering if she passed out again.

"Aviella?" I ask, struggling to keep the desperation to hear her out of my voice.

"Yeah," she says, so softly I strain to hear her. "We'll see."

"We'll see? What do you mean? You know they're not going to sit by and leave us here."

She sighs heavily but doesn't say more. I'm left waiting again, listening to her breathing which sounds like its hitching. There's no doubt she has broken ribs at the very least.

"I'm sorry, Luca," she says. "It's all coming to a head."

"Sure, but we'll figure it out," I say, forcing more cheer into my words than I'm feeling.

A lock clicks and a distant door screeches as its forced open. Footsteps click on the metal floor, coming closer. I press myself tighter to the window straining to see who is coming. Even with the cold-iron magical symbols separating my magic from me I'm still aware of the power walking towards us. It's oppressive, suffocating almost.

Two of the red-robed guards come into view, and now they're carrying assault rifles instead of stun sticks. They march grimly past, but the source of the oppression isn't them. The guards take up positions against the far wall, but I still can't see who they're bringing with them.

"She's here," a familiar voice says. It's He Who Has Risen talking to someone.

"We shall see," another voice says.

"No, I'm right. This one will identify her for me, you'll see," He Who Has Risen says.

I can't see the speakers yet, but the tone of He Who Has Risen's voice is propitiating, almost begging. It's strange. I've heard his voice so much over the loudspeakers before I got myself thrown into the lower floor, and it's always been filled with certainty and self-confidence. None of that is what I'm hearing now.

The footsteps come closer, then two more guards walk past my small field of vision. These two are dressed in flashy green suits with dark sunglasses. Their faces glint, reflecting the dim light in the hall. When one of them passes directly in front of my small window, I see the cause. Scales. They have scales on their skin.

He turns and looks directly at me, and even through his dark sunglasses, his eyes burn red. He grins revealing sharp, pointy teeth that look fit for tearing apart raw meat. My blood turns cold as he marches past, and then the cold turns to solid ice.

He Who Has Risen has his image pasted everywhere in the bunker, so I recognize him. He at least looks like a normal human. He's tall, gaunt, and pale with a yellow tint to his eyes but nothing overly pronounced, a bad diet is all. Not that it's uncommon in the Apocalypse to have a bad diet. It's actually more the norm.

It's not him who causes the chills or makes my stomach drop. A step behind He Who Has Risen, another man comes into view. He's tall with long dirty-blonde hair that's swept aside in a half-done part. He's tanned with a few days' growth of beard, and he's wearing a black turtleneck. He glances over, and his eyes are the most shocking, rich green, like the rolling hills of Ireland. He pauses, his eyes locking onto mine and the world fades away.

Casmir.

When I meet his gaze I can't deny the fear. The last of the dragons. His high forehead wrinkles as he frowns, then takes a step closer to the door.

"He's extra," He Who Has Risen says, "he's not the important one. She's over here."

"I'll decide who is important," Casmir says.

He doesn't raise his voice at all. When he speaks it's more a whisper, but one that is so clear everyone can hear it. He taps a finger against his lips and narrows his eyes.

"You might actually have something," Casmir says.

"I do!" the Prophet exclaims excitedly. "I told you I do, and I do."

Casmir turns and walks away. I can barely make him out stopping in front of Aviella's door. I'm so focused on trying to see what he's doing, I almost miss the next thing. Another person walks through the guards and comes to stand next to Casmir.

"Is this her?" Casmir asks, turning to the newcomer.

"It is," Efram says, nodding.

"Efram?" I cry out. "What are you doing?"

He doesn't look my way, his shoulders are slumped, and his head bowed.

"Interesting," Casmir says. "Well, my little experiment. You've certainly panned out."

"Thank you, sir," the Prophet says, all but bouncing from foot to foot.

"Bring her," Casmir says, turning and walking away.

"No!" I yell. "You sons of bitches, no. It's not her. Efram? Tell them, it's not her!"

Efram's head hangs lower if that is even possible, and he rushes out of my sight. I grab the bars of my door and strain to break them. They don't budge. I can't reach my magic to enhance my strength. I'm stuck.

Aviella is pulled out of her cell, all but dragged by the creepy new guards in green suits. She looks up at me as she is roughly shoved past. She smiles.

"I love you," she mouths before they drag her away.

I scream and throw myself against the door trying to break it down.

CHAPTER FORTY-THREE

AVIELLA

I knew it was coming to this. It doesn't make it any easier though. Damn, it hurts so much. I'm dragged through the halls by the new guards. The Prophet and Casmir have disappeared, leaving me to the not-gentle ministrations of the guards.

I try to separate myself from it, but I can't reach the astral anymore. The collar on my neck keeps the magic out of reach. It's like there's glass between me and it. It's frustrating in itself but made worse because I really don't want this experience.

I know this is the path, though. I'm sure of it. All the signs and the twists in the road have led me here. I'm not going to be the one to save my Dad, but I can save the world. I think. God, I hope I'm right. If not... well here goes nothing, right?

They hose me down with water hoses then force me into a loose-fitting white robe before dragging me out into the public areas of the bunker. Four guards flank me. Crowds of people close around us shouting, jeering. It's not so bad until the first piece of food hits me. It smells awful, a rotten something or other that stains the robes.

It's like the floodgates open. I'm pelted from all sides, and the crowd closes in. I'm hit from all sides. They're screaming about how I'm a heretic and unclean. It's crazy. They're all but frothing at the mouth. The guards try to hold them back, but they're insane.

I'm dragged through until at last we go through a door, and the rabid crowds are closed outside. The guards drag me back to my feet and shove me forward. I stumble and drop to my knees in front of the Prophet and Casmir. My head hurts and is too heavy to hold up. Forcing myself to look up, I see Efram standing behind Casmir. The pain on his face makes my heart break. He won't meet my eyes, but I reach a hand towards him, wanting to offer him comfort.

"This is it!" the Prophet says. "She's the one that the Shadow wants. She is the power of twelve!"

"Perhaps," Casmir says.

"So," I say, coughing to clear my throat, blood drops to the floor. "What's up with you two? Old lost lovers?"

"You can't speak to him like that!" the Prophet screeches.

"Clearly not," Casmir says. "He is but an experiment, interesting enough, but still an experiment."

"I am the One Who Is Risen! I went to the other side, I came back," the Prophet sputters, spewing his own line of bullshit.

"Right," I say, shaking my head. "He Who Has Risen, got it. You buy your own hype."

"It's not hype! None of the others survived, only me! I died, but I returned!"

"Congratulations," I say. "You're still a moron."

A fist hits me so fast I drop to the ground, stars exploding in my head.

"Where are her twelve?" Casmir asks.

"I don't have twelve. I don't even have one." I spit out more blood and what looks like part of a tooth.

"She does, too!" the Prophet says. "She's the one."

"Sorry, not it," I say, arms shaking with the effort of holding my head off the floor.

"Are they here?" Casmir asks.

"Yes," the Prophet says confidently.

"Interesting," Casmir says, kneeling in front of me.

He touches my chin, gently lifting until my eyes meet his. His touch is warm, and his magic dances just outside my reach. It's an invitation and damn but it'd be nice to take it in. Magic could heal my wounds, set me free, but that's not the path, is it? The path demands a sacrifice. That's the one thing that history and all my journey so far has taught me, there's always a price. The only question is, who's going to pay it?

He's a sexy man, and I see the connection between him and his brothers. As we stare into each other's eyes, I know, with total certainty, he's the twelfth. He doesn't yet, but I do. If only I'd found him sooner. His face shimmers and the mark of Shadow flickers on his forehead. He's still being manipulated. I wish I'd had time to set you free, Casmir. I'd like to have known you.

"It's not me," I say, blood dripping down my chin onto his hand.

"A test then," he says, rising and letting my head drop. It's all I can do to keep it from bouncing off the floor.

"A test, yes, a test," the Prophet says. "But what test?"

"Put her up outside, with your other unclean. If she is the power of twelve, then her mates will come to rescue her. Then we'll know, won't we?" Casmir says.

"Oh!" the Prophet exclaims.

"NO!" Efram yells, rushing forward.

Casmir doesn't turn to meet his attack, merely gestures behind himself and Efram freezes then is lifted off the ground. He slowly drifts through the air until he's hovering next to me.

"One," Casmir says. "I think this experiment is off to an interesting start."

"Don't... hurt... him," I force the words while fighting my way to my feet.

Efram drops to the floor in a heap. He struggles to get off the floor, and his eyes meet mine, begging. The despair on his face breaks my heart. I hate putting him through this, but the price has to be paid. Saving the world is going to require a sacrifice, and I can't choose one of them.

The only thing I can do is smile. I've no doubt it's not as reassuring as my intention for it, blood is pouring out of my mouth and nose, left eye is swelling shut, but it's all I can do for him. He shakes his head.

"Let it be me," he says. "Please, Aviella, don't do this."

"No... choice," I say, heaving breath with each word.

It's so hard to breathe. Every inhale is sharp pain. The guards come closer. Magic pulses close, so close I should be able to touch it, but this is part of the price to pay. I can't let her win. The Shadow must lose, I have to save not only my guys, but all of them. I can't let another bunker fall or another innocent, lost soul to be taken by the Shadow.

I'm pulled up to my feet. I try to stand but my legs are too weak, so they drag me through the corridors. It seems like forever since we entered New Jerusalem. It hasn't been that long though, I do have to admit I've lost track of time. It all blurs together when everything hurts.

The speakers tucked around the upper floors are calling for everyone to gather. Great, I guess there's going to be a show. Unfortunately for me, I'm the star of it.

"Aviella!" Silas yells.

I barely spot him in the crowd, fighting his way through, but they hold him back. The doors to the bunker open, and the light outside is harsh, blindingly bright. I close my eyes and let the ride happen as they drag me outside.

This is all part of it. I do my best to relax, because there's nothing else for it. Eyes closed, my attention is drawn to a golden warmth in my core. It's nice, like a cozy fire. As I pay attention to it, the warmth spreads through my limbs and it pushes away the pain.

This is not so bad after all. I'll ride along like this and soon it will all be over. Images of my boys drift through my thoughts. Each of them unique and special, each their own and each mine. Tynan, Alaric, Shen the three dragons whom I feel approaching even now. They're not going to make it but that's okay, if they did, they'd screw this up. Tynan would never accept that this is the way it has to be.

Nathanial and Rafe. Nate is close, I feel him approaching. He'll understand. He has to. Rafe is distant, reaching for me but he's not close enough to understand what's happening. Something is holding him back. He'll be all right though, Rafe is strong. Stronger than even he realizes, I think. How many demons have taken a stand against the Shadow? Not many I would think, and yet Rafe has.

Luca is still trapped in the cell down below. He's screaming, throwing himself against the door over and over. I want to reach out and calm him and somehow, I manage to get something past the barrier. Magically touching him and he stops hurting himself. It's not worth it, he's going to need his strength.

His brethren, Gavin, Ronan, and sweet Killian only now are becoming aware which is good, if they knew before they'd charge in and screw it all up.

And Efram. Poor sweet Efram. In so many ways I'm closer to him than the others. I hope they understand. He's dragged to the front of the crowd forming a circle around me. Three guards on him, a rune bound iron collar on his neck now as well. The crowd swells, cheering, chanting but it's all distant.

My body is laid out on the wooden frame. This is going to hurt, I know it, but it doesn't seem to really affect me here in the golden warmth. I bask in it, letting it keep the pain at bay.

"Aviella!" Silas screams but at the same time the pain in both my hands explodes.

Golden light bursts apart conscious thought. Damn it. I'm screaming but even my own voice is distant, not really me. It's happening to someone else, right? As my thoughts reform towards coherency they're blown apart again by pain in my feet, then they break my legs.

"Mom," I whisper. "Please…"

The warmth pulses, embracing me as it pushes the agony away. I'm lifted into the air and the weight of my body pulls down on the points I'm pinned to the wood.

Casmir and the Prophet walk out of the crowd, appearing in front of me. Casmir's gaze is studious, interested, like he's watching only to learn. Curiosity on his face as he waits to see what will happen. I try to meet his gaze, to be brave, but putting that much effort into it makes me too aware of the pain.

I let my head drop and retreat into the golden warmth. I drift for… I don't know how long. The crowds are still here. Casmir is watching closely. Silas is now kneeling next to Efram below me with a collar of his own on.

Suddenly the smell of sulfur is on the air and there are screams. A tear forms over the crowd opening to reveal fiery red and blackness. Rafe explodes out of the rip, black bat wings holding him up in the air. He's in full-on demonic mode. I've never seen him like this before, but I would know him anywhere.

"Aviella!" he screams, driving himself forward.

He's almost to me when the nets land on him. They glow with green-purple magic, entangling his wings and pulling him to the ground. He fights, but in the end, there is no hope for a rescue. There can't be. I'm the sacrifice.

I had to make the choice. One of them, or me. Someone had to pay the price it would take to save this world. It is our one hope, a wing and a prayer for sure, but what other choice was there? This is what had to happen, and I couldn't choose one of them.

So this is it. Me.

I see Nathanial floating in the air a distance away, watching, but the pain and agony on his face makes it clear that he's being held back by Divine will. I force a smile for him, but it only makes the pain on his face worse.

It's almost time. Only a little bit more and this will be over.

The crowd is on their knees praising the false prophet, but they'll soon see. They have to see he's false. The Shadow has to know that I'll do whatever it takes.

In the crowd I see her, walking through them, unnoticed. She locks eyes with me, her head tilting to one side, lips pursing. She's beautiful. Stunningly so. A half smile is on her face, but in her eyes is something else. She knows what this means. She knows, and she's scared? Worried? It's hard to tell with something like her, but it gives me comfort to see it.

It's time.

The dragons are cresting the hill. I feel their presence before I see them but an instant later their shapes are on the horizon. The mages teleport in, appearing at my feet, ready for battle. They're not alone. Oh god, Rowan is with them!

She looks up, her eyes wide, horrified at what she sees. She reaches up to me with glowing hands, power pulsing off of her in waves while the mages form a protective circle around her. They're trying to save me, but they can't. It has to run its course.

I'm lifting out and away, the golden warmth pulling me along with it. There's only one last thing to do.

"I... forgive... you... ALL," I say as my last breath exhales.

A deafening trumpet sounds.

All the world is torn apart.

Hang in there with me, this isn't the end! I promise it gets better and it'll all be worth it. The *Power of Twelve* series concludes with the final book, **Apocalypse the Battlefield**

ABOUT THE AUTHOR

USA Today Bestselling Author of fantasy and scifi romance, Miranda Martin's books feature larger than life heroes with out-of-this-world anatomy and smart heroines destined to save the world. As a little girl she would sneak off with her nose in a book, dreaming of magical realms. Today she brings those fantasies to life and adores every fan who chooses to live in them for a while.

She was born and raised in southern Virginia, but as a veteran she's traveled to places like Korea, Hawaii and good 'ole Texas. Now she's settled in Kansas, the heart of America, with her husband and daughters. Her favorite animals are dragons, unicorns and cats. If she's not writing, you can still find her tucked away somewhere with a warm blanket and her nose in a book.

Get in touch!
mirandamartinromance.com
miranda@mirandamartinromance.com

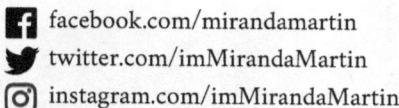

facebook.com/mirandamartin
twitter.com/imMirandaMartin
instagram.com/imMirandaMartin

ALSO BY MIRANDA MARTIN

Red Planet Dragon's of Tajss Series
Red Planet Jungle Series
The Power of Twelve Series
The Alva Series
Dragon's & Phoenixes Series